A Dreamer's Secret

Dedicated to
Marianela
Mi Abuela

Acknowledgments

I would like to thank my parents Orlando and Elizabeth for raising me to be the person I am now. My pain in the butt brothers Josh and Christian for making me a stronger person. My Abuela and Abuelo, you continue to teach me every day.

To my Tia Grettel, you always push me to be better and believe I can do anything I set my mind to. You're the light in everyone's lives and I am blessed to be, your bug.

To my cousin Frankie, you motivate and inspire others. Thanks for being more then blood. To my Alabama family, I love you!

To my girls, CLC Forever! Nicole, you always encouraged me to not give up on my writing and always helped me keep my creativity at the surface. To my fabulous Oliver, my partner in crime and in song. To the youth leaders who shaped us. To my other family, Raul, Gloria, Carlos and Jason. Thanks for the love, tons of laughs and encouragement.

Acknowledgments

And to the boy that drove me so crazy, it made me a writer.

Thank you to my Fiancé, whom still loves me spite my obsession with fantasy, and its characters, and the strings that come with that.

My fur babies, Paulie and Bashful, you make every day worth it with your unconditional puppy love.

Last but not least, thank you Jesus Christ for all your blessings on this earth. All these people in my life are an example of your love.

Seth – Means, "Placed or appointed" in Hebrew. From the Greek form of Egyptian it means "pillar or dazzle".

"And we know that all things work together for good to those who love God, Too those who are the called according to his purpose."

– Romans 8:28

"Set me as a seal upon your heart. As a seal upon your arm; for love is as strong as death, Jealousy as cruel as the grave; its flames are flames of fire, a most vehement flame. Many waters cannot quench love, nor can the floods drown it." – Song of Solomon 8:6-7

Inspired by true events

Preface

"I'm really scared." I said with a small voice. I was lying in my little cotton bed in a big cold room that I seemed to never get used to. My blanket was thin and a little scratchy against my skin. It was dark and there was a storm outside, like most nights. I could hear the wind whooshing by and the tree branches hitting the window by my bed. The lightning was bright through the window to, and the thunder seemed to vibrate the whole orphanage.
 It smelled a bit of must and peanut butter.

   "Seth, Seth wake up its scary!" I started to scream for the second time at the top of my lungs, now with tears running down my face.

 "Shut up Riley!" whispered some of the other kids in the

room. I sniffled and took a deep breath to try and calm down.

Then as I began my next cry I felt someone climbing into my bed.

"Seth, is that you?"

"Shhh yes it's me, you are okay now it's safe."

He assured me with his little soothing boy voice. He crawled into the bed next to me and put his arms around my stomach. I turned to look at him, his small blue eyes shined in the darkness, they always relaxed me when I was frightened. He wiped the stupid long tears from my face. "It's okay Riley, I'm right here." He whispered into my ear. I smiled and let out a small sigh of relief.

"Seth do you think someone will adopt us one day?"

"I don't know, maybe." He replied.

"But what if someone takes you? Then you won't be with me anymore and I'll be alone."

"I won't ever leave you, we are in this together, I'm not leaving and neither are you."

"Unless were together? I asked.

"Yes."

"You both are such babies!" Shouted Bobby from across the room. The lights suddenly flashed on and everyone was beginning to wake up and whine. Seth and I both crawled out of the bed. Bobby was always mean to everyone here. He had brown eyes and short brown hair. Kind of like a mushroom, he was chubby to. He walked over to me and began teasing me like he did every day. "You're going to be here forever and I bet Seth's going to leave you too and not care."

"Shut up Bobby!" I screamed in sudden anger at his words. He then grabbed me by my hair and yanked me to the floor. I squealed and cried out in pain. Seth shouted with rage and jumped on top of Bobby and began punching him.

I could hear the thunder louder now and the other kids chanting, "Fight, fight, fight." Bobby was now somehow punching Seth down to the floor.

I curled up in a ball and cried, "Please stop! Seth please!" There was a big slam and Ms. Woods ran in shouting and grabbed Bobby away from Seth. I stood up and hugged Seth.

"What are you brats doing!?" She asked with anger in her voice.

"Seth's not sleeping in his bed." Bobby said annoyingly and pointed his finger at us. I wanted to bite it so bad until he cried.

Ms. Woods yelled some more.

"All of you to bed now or you're getting no playground time in the morning!" At the thought of that everyone ran back to their beds quietly, even Bobby. She walked over and pulled Seth away from me and pushed him towards his bed. She muttered more and turned the lights back off slamming the door behind her.

I crawled in my bed and curled up. I couldn't help it but

begin to cry myself to sleep. I also felt like throwing up now, I had upset my stomach, which happened a lot. I tried to focus on something that made me happy as I drifted off to sleep.

When I woke up in the morning, Seth was sleeping right next to me with his hand resting where Bobby had yanked on my hair. My heart fluttered with joy and I smiled and thought, *Seth was my best friend in the whole world and he would always be mine…*

∞

1. The Love Cards

The citizens of the city fled through the streets in horror. Their terror stricken faces screamed for help in the restless city of New York. As the police cars roared by there were sirens coming from every direction trying to reach the scene of mishap. A bullet was fired from one of the alleys and it made people scream even more...

She was high up, almost as if she was on the tallest building that had ever existed. He had swooped her up and saved her from the evil villain down below, she was unsure of how she got there. Did he fly? Did he use a rope or arrow to come down with? Was he masked or hooded? He stood in the dark shadows of the night. She could not make out a face but she knew it was the hero that would save the city. She looked down, a fire had begun at a building not too far from theirs. People were waving their hands in the air for help. She glanced over at him, wondering if he was going to help the people that were about to be burned alive.

Down below there were people looking up at the burning building. They looked like they were wondering if the rescue would come in time or if people were going to start jumping out the windows so they would not burn to death. Some people kept fleeing the scene afraid of what they might see. Others stopped and watched in shock. Just moments later, a woman was falling from the building, the crowd gasped in dismay. Suddenly right before she hit the pavement, something stopped her fall and she was safely standing on the sidewalk. The citizens looked around for an explanation. More people were appearing safe and unharmed on the streets. *She took a step closer to him, there was a lot of fog in the air which made it hard to make anything out about this strange hero. She admired the skylines of the beautiful New York City. It was breath taking every time she was outside her apartment walls. The sound of cars and busses driving by down below. The smoke rising up from the sewers on the streets. The sound of sirens from a distance got closer. It seemed like his face was about to appear into her vision, but instead he fled swiftly in the smoke and was gone. She did not know how he disappeared so fast, it was almost magical…*

*

...I pulled the green hood of my sweater over my head to cover my hair from the rain, I don't really know why I did, I didn't care if I got wet, the rain was sweet on my skin. Maybe I just felt it was an excuse to hide myself as best as possible without looking like the weirdo I already was. I walked out of my small apartment door and down the brick steps. I threw my bag over my neck so it could hang on me as securely as I could make it. Living in New York no one ever knew when someone might run past you, seconds later with your belongings. The big storm had passed but there was still a slight drizzle.

The sun still hid behind the clouds, kind of like I was hiding at that moment. I walked as fast as I could through the people on the streets. I could still hear the buzzing from my alarm clock that woke me from the dream about a vigilante. That is what I get for falling asleep when there's a marathon of superhero movies on television. I could not even remember which part was a dream or the movie.

The scenery after a storm here was just perfect, it didn't stop the buzzing of taxi's though, or how fast people seemed to walk without getting hit by a car or bumping into others. You become an expert when you have been in this city long enough. I kept to the side of the sidewalk till I came to a crossing, I watched as a googly-eyed couple walked by me, giggling and whispering to each other, his arm around her waist and her head rested upon his shoulder, their hands

15

intertwined like a vine. I stared until they turned out of sight.

Oh crap, you're probably thinking, *is this story going to be about love!* Well I hate to disappoint you but yes it is. But don't shut the book just yet, it gets worse.

Boyfriends and girlfriends, dating, the whole stupid concept. Like children with game cards, they just get traded around, torn, scratched and everyone just does it over and over till they find a better one and then the cycle continues. I'm not just saying teenagers; ten year olds are apparently in love nowadays. It just grossed me out. So since being an outcast to humanity I had a different more complicating and pathetic situation, but we'll get into that later…

I live with my best friend in the whole world, my dog, Jackie. She's a Pitbull terrier mix, the best dog ever. Jack I call her for short, I love that name even though she's a female, Jack fit her well. I saved her from a shelter before they put her to sleep for no reason, but that there was no room there. I pushed the big blue door open to my college and walked inside. After an argument with myself, I finally took the hood off and let my long black hair out, the bangs fell in my face.

Student's shuffled through the halls chatting with one another. I passed a few guys laughing real hard in a corner and two girls stood watching from a short distance pointing at them as they giggled. I reached my locker, even though this was college and no one really had lockers unless they

16

bought them; since I carried so much stuff on me I had one.

I opened it up to see the pictures of my friends I had taped to the door. I smiled, no one could look at these pictures and not. I unzipped my sweater and threw it inside. Underneath I wore a green t-shirt and blue jeans. I leaned against the locker; my arms crossed and glanced at the pictures again. There was one of my two best friends, Abigail and Kayleen, but I call them Abby and Kay. Their cousins and live together. We also live in walking distance which was pretty awesome. They're my best girls, my sunshine on a rainy day. We have been a trio since the end of middle school. Through all our good times and bad, but we got out still strong.

Abby and I have a lot of things in common, from the hobby side of things, Abby's more of a congenial type of girl.

She has blonde shoulder length hair, her skin is a honey glow, and her eyes are a cute hazel. She's the tallest out of the trio, but also average for her age. Long athletic legs and very petite, though she doesn't work for it or engage in any sport for it, doesn't ever gain a pound no matter what she eats.

Now Kay, she's the more wild one, but also one of a kind, she's loud and acts like a five year old most of the time, and then it grows on us and then soon were all acting like kids.

Kay also loves to sing and dance, no matter where she is, she could be in the middle of the pointless mall or at a funeral. She will just dance. Her hair is an auburn color, curly and short as well. Her eyes are dark brown and her skin a creamy cocoa. She's average height and weight. In the picture the three of us were laughing and sitting under a tree, I think we were at central park that day. I noticed fingers snapping in front of me.

"Hello Riley wake up," Abby stood over me smiling big.

"Oh hey I didn't notice you, I'm used to hearing the screaming and laughing from the distance before I actually see you".

"Yeah or me!" came Kay's voice from behind Abby. I stuck my tongue out at them.

Kay whined on some more.

"What is it with you Rie? You're always spacing out on us." Abby asked.

"It's kind of weird," and then she went into one of her, "Kay moments" and started saying the word over and over again in different tones … "weird, weird, weird." I stared at her. "Weird, weird, ok I'm done ha-ha, stop staring at me Rie you know that freaks me out." She stopped and laughed at herself.

I was born with these light blue almost silver eyes, with such big pupils so they stood out. They were kind of like husky eyes. I liked the way they looked against my long black hair and tan skin. Though I hated the stares I sometimes got.

"Ok let's get to class." I said to them as we started walking down the long hallway. Moments later I stopped. "Oh wait I left my English book, I'll be right back".

I turned and ran back down the hallway for the second time.
I found my locker and quickly grabbed the book, as I did
that my eyes scanned the pictures again, there was one of me
and Jack and then one of me and Seth.

Seth is the closest friend I've had since before I could
remember. We met when we were really little, I was just
about four or five years old and Seth a year older than me.
We have been best buds since, well at least to me. He is that
typical guy, the one all the girls seem to fall in love with
right away. In a movie when he walked in the room the
music would start and he would walk in slow motion while
a fan made his hair flow in the air and he would smile wide.
Literally.

A lot of girls fell for his amazing charm. I guess if they
didn't then there was something wrong with them.

What I did like was that if asked I could say, *oh yea I know
him, that's my friend Seth!* If a girl was asking me the
response is something like, *oh you're so lucky!* With a little
drool possibly hanging down there jaw. But the honest truth
was, I was not. I was in worse than any of those girls. Why?
You might ask, well because I hate to admit it once again in
my mind but, because I was that one girl who fell in love
with him… The love that happened mostly just in books.
The love I wished desperately to not even feel.
It haunted me instead.

I stared at the picture some more, we were at some

arcade playing a video game and laughing are heads off. Him with his perfect features and then me, *EW*, I thought. I focused on him instead, him with his breathtaking dark blue eyes. Just like lapis lazuli, I learned that color just last week, the most beautiful shade of blue there could be, and Seth's jet black short hair. Perfect muscles and over that was the best olive colored skin. Seth is, we assumed Greek and Egyptian, but I don't think anyone knows, but either way he's perfectly beautiful.

Imagine that! But this isn't about his looks, didn't even start with them. I never had thought of him that way at first, he was just my funny looking, goofy friend. But now the way I felt for him sometimes felt like a sin, unhealthy, he was my drug. I couldn't ever get rid of him because I loved him too much to even try and get the venom he has in me out. In a way I liked it, no matter the pain.

He didn't know I cared this much, and will never know how I feel. He's thought of me as one of his buddies, never just another girl he knew and forgot. I would not let that happen.

You might think, *Wow why are guys like that? Are they blind?* But that wasn't the case. I wasn't waiting for him to realize I loved him.

I was waiting to see if he maybe with so much doubt would end up loving me. Fat chance, but that was my wait. If not then oh well, still haven't lost him. I didn't want him to know and my biggest fear in life was that, if he did figure it out.

Everyone has a secret I'm told, this was mine. Something that still shocks me to this day is that I never found Seth attractive till I was much older. I just melted into his personality and heart, and somehow he's beautiful to me now, one day, my eyes just burst open to him.
His soul, spirit and mind, were what I wanted the most, I longed just to know how his soul felt and what his mind thought. I couldn't live with the thought of losing him over my stupid overbearing feelings. It hurt just thinking about it now.

Somehow keeping it to myself felt as if the love I had for him was stronger than ever, because hiding it just gained it power, never weakened it. No matter how much I wanted to be with him, I couldn't. Not that way. But this way I was with him and I had won in my own way. I was keeping it that way by not screwing it up.
Seth and I pretty much have the same story, both our parents died when we were babies and then we were brought to the orphanage. We agreed we did not care to look into our past, we were told that our files were lost in a fire. So when we were old enough or ran away, I'm not so sure which story we stuck with. There was nothing for us to even look for when we were free. I suddenly snapped out of my memory daze and came back to reality.
"Hey Rie", came the smooth and gentle quiet voice from behind me. I sucked in my breath and automatically spun

around grabbing the book and slamming the door.

I cringed to the sound, *very smooth*. I told myself.

"Hey", I replied panicked all of a sudden. *Where are my words?* I had to think straight but even if I did no good words came out. "What's up?" I added, feeling like hiding inside the locker now.

I then made a big mistake, I looked up at him. I tried to just look at his black t-shirt and blue jeans that he seemed to look amazing in, but I gave in and gazed up at his face, those eyes gazed down at me with some unknown tease or slyness, my whole brain went fuzzy.

I shook my thoughts and smiled, because that's all we ever did, was smile at each other, I had no words and he was just Seth. "Nothing much, just spending a lot of time with my girlfriend, work, the usual." I kept smiling at him as my stomach tightened like I had been kicked repeatedly. "That's great, I'm happy for you". I replied. I really was.

"And you? He asked still smiling at me with his big beautiful eyes that I couldn't seem to look away from.

I lied to everyone when they asked me how I was or what I had been up to lately. I didn't want to lie to Seth, he was the only person it hurt so much to lie to. But I wasn't really lying just not telling the whole truth, sure I'm fine and no, the same as always nothing really new, was my repeated response.

I'm not sure what people wanted to hear, I was the most

boring person. I didn't even want to be around myself.
He nodded his head and then gave me the see you later look.
I watched him walk away, he had to be out of sight for me to
be able to think straight again. He ran his fingers through his
hair, the last thing I saw was his small tattoo of flames
sticking out above the back of his neck. I regained my
thoughts, words and air and made my way down the hall
once again.

*

The clock ticked on so slow, it had to be just a few minutes
and this dreaded class would be over. "So does anyone
know what this means?" asked Mr. Smith our math teacher.
Explaining something about numbers and graphs and trying
to relate it to life.

"I do!" announced Sophie, the preppy redhead who
always has the answer. I was sitting in the middle row Abby
on one side and Kay on the other. In front of me was Paige,
besides Abby and Kay she was another close friend. Brown
hair with glasses and light skin, she's French with a real cool
accent. She's real athletic and a good movie buddy.

Then there was her boyfriend Sean, he has glasses too
and athletic. Tan with curly short gold hair and green eyes.
He and the other guys are mostly Seth's friends, I don't hang
out or talk with them much. But there lots of fun, Vince with
his goofy personality with shortcut blondish brown hair and

gray-green eyes and Michael with his nice and quiet temper, he's bald with very green eyes, muscular and well-tanned he's short but really sweet to everyone, smart too.

There's the last two of our group even though I barely see them. They are Belinda and Sonny, very opposites. Belinda's Spanish with long brown hair also quite and nice, everyone wants Michael and her together, they both are a lot alike. She's very talented too, and then there's Sonny, the crazy shopaholic blonde, who's obsessed with boys, but she's funny and her happy go-luckiness sometimes rubs onto you.

"Alright class dismissed", Mr. Smith announced.
I looked up from my doodles of stick men when he spoke.
I hadn't heard a word he taught, my mind seemed to wonder so easily, I thought of what Seth was doing, maybe sleeping in his class. I stood up grabbing my stuff and turned my phone on.
" Hey Riley, you going to the party tonight?" it was Vince asking.

"Umm, not sure who's going?" I asked.
"Everyone!" Said Paige standing up in front of me fixing her glasses.
"You should come." Sonny said.
"I'm sure there will be some hot guys there, you could use a little romance in your life your always alone, and well don't you want a boyfriend?"

There she goes again, I thought.

"No Sonny I'm just fine."

Michael gave me a remorse expression.

"I'm fine guy's geez!"

Sonny continued. "Have you ever even had a boyfriend? A date? Or even any kind of closeness with a male?"

I replied a little annoyed now.

"No and I'm getting tired of this conversation, I'm leaving and I don't know guys, you know parties are just not my scene."

"I'll take that as a no." Sonny added before changing the conversation back, I ignored her.

"You can just come to hangout, you don't have to do anything you don't want to, and come on it will be fun." Michael was so sweet to me.

"Aw thanks Michael, I'll think about it." I was getting really sick of this classroom so I quickly made my way out now with them all laughing and chatting behind me. Not watching where I was going I bumped right into someone. *Dang it! How did he get over here? He seemed to be everywhere.*

"Hey watch where you're going short stuff."

"Hey I am not that short!" I said with a fake frown.

"Meany!" I added trying to control my sudden sped up heartbeat.

"Oh I'm sorry," he said patting my head.

"Stop it Seth!" We both laughed, we teased with each other a lot.

"You going tonight?" He asked me.

"Oh you're going, umm I think I might."

Ooh now you want to go Riley! I heard a voice in my head say.

"Good, because it would be so boring without you." Seth said making me smile again. He patted my head and walked away as he chuckled under his breath, I rolled my eyes. *Oh great see what you did.*

*

The music was deafeningly loud, I was standing with Abby and Kay by the snack table at Sean's house, we were arguing over which movie we were going to see after the party. I wanted to see a thriller but Kay wanted to see a comedy and Abby didn't care, but she had to choose one to make it an even vote. She was stubborn like that, never took sides, but how else would we decide.

"Okay how about we flip a coin?" I asked starting to lose my concentration.

"Oh good idea!" Abby blurted out, excited only because we would not be arguing anymore.

"Heads or tails?" Asked Kay reaching into her purse to find a penny. My eyes drifted passed them to a couple in another corner. I had sudden flashes of this couple in my head. Not sure if they were memories, dreams or horrified images of

26

what the future might hold. I always tried not to picture them because it just made my stomach sick.

"It does not matter you pick." I said really distracted and tense now, I really tried not to look that way and to focus on what I was doing or saying.

I was weak.

I do not even remember who won, I just didn't care anymore. I smiled and agreed to everything my friends were saying while I struggled to act natural even as I cussed at myself for being so stupid, for feeling like this and letting these silly images consume me.

I didn't pay attention to her, I never did, she was like the person blurred out on a cop show. I just looked at him and how happy and calm he seemed.

He's never going to look at you like that you know, said the controlling voice in my head.

I know, I replied to myself.

Well I always have to remind you!!

I replied to myself once more.

Don't ever stop, you have to keep crushing my hope.

He glanced over at me and our eyes locked for a second, those eyes of his were like pretty Christmas lights, one glimpse is all you need to help you off your feet, to bring sudden joy to your sadness. I loved Christmas and the feeling I got when I saw the bright lights on the buildings, houses and trees. Well at least to me. It seemed like a good way to describe how his eyes made me feel, even though it still didn't feel good enough, I swear his eyes sometimes changed shades too.

It was the best sensation in the world, his dark blue eyes. I turned away as he did and focused on something else, he was happy and that's what mattered, it was okay if those eyes weren't looking at me, as long as they were colorful, happy and bright.

The party went on in a slur hazy illusion. It was okay at moments, like when I grabbed my friends and ran out of the house to, *'go on an adventure and explore the neighborhood,'* to me I just wanted to get the hell out of there and breathe. I was pretty sure the movie was a comedy, I did not remember much of the movie. I laughed when everyone else laughed, it even distracted me a few times, but I just wasn't that into it. My insides ached and I felt nauseas and just wanted to go home and be alone. Maybe there I could be more in tune of everything that was really going on in reality.

∞

2. Sweet intruder

I stood outside gazing up at the dark blue sky like I did even in reality. This was where I liked it best; I did not feel pain here. I wasn't confused or upset; I was free in a different world and the emotions I felt were not as painful physically and unhealthy, than the usual.

It was a late and chilly night. It was so dark, there were lots of stars shining bright in the sky to see.

I was wearing red sweatpants and a white old ripped up t-shirt.

I stood as lost in thought as I gazed up at the sky wondering exactly where I was. I suddenly spun around to the sound of a snap of a twig from behind me. I looked over to where the sound had come from but could not see anything, the fence turned the corner around the tall brick house I seemed to be at.

This wasn't my small apartment in NYC, but in this dream this was my house and I seemed to know it very well. Maybe it was just a stray cat or raccoon. I thought, they always go looking through my trash cans at night.

I turned again to the sound of crunchy noises you only heard when someone was slowly walking on grass and trying not to disturb it, this person was not so good at it.

I reached over and grabbed a metal pole I kept hidden by the fence. Then I called out. "Hey is anyone there?"

I could hear a low snickering, was this intruder laughing at me! Well he won't be when I smack him in the head.

"Listen, don't try anything stupid".

"Shh, calm down it's me." The voice cut me off.

"Seth! Is that you?" I asked now whispering into the darkness. I still had the pole raised in defense mode pointing towards the voice.

"Yea Rie, you can calm down, no need to stab anyone tonight".

He laughed more, this time louder.

I did too and tossed the pole away.

"Wait, you are the one sneaking around in my backyard, what the hell are you doing here? It's three AM!" I harshly whispered to the bits of him I could see in the dark.

"I think I should ask you what you are doing up this late?"

"I need to talk to you." He added quickly.

My heart was now beating uneasily.

What was he doing here so late in the night?

I shivered at the thought.

"What's up?" I asked him walking closer because I needed to see him and have him as close as my mind would allow.

"And just so you know, you could use the front door."

"True." He replied.

"I could, but it wouldn't have been as exciting and I got to see you with a pole ready to attack, that was worth it."

I laughed, "Okay what's on your mind that's so urgent it couldn't wait till the morning?"

"Well there's something I need to tell you." He continued slowly talking as he walked closer to me, reaching my limit of closeness.

And then I went into a small panic mode.

"Seth what's wrong? Are you ok? Did something happen?"

I tend to get overly dramatic; I got to get better at that. I thought to myself.

"I'm fine, relax woman." He said showing me his arms and spinning around like a model, and he did it all too well in a goofy way, which made me laugh again.

"No one hurts this beautiful beast."

"Ha nope never, okay then what's wrong?" He got serious again and I got that sudden feeling of non-reality sinking in.

"Okay listen and listen good, there's something I been needing to tell you and it's weird I don't know why I feel this way, it's almost confusing, but I think it's just because... well ...I don't know I think I like you ... a lot ... I mean, I think I love you, and I know it sounds crazy but it seems as if you've been waiting for me or something, I know I sound so stupid. I'm not someone who waits so long to tell someone something, because I could lose you forever and I don't want that."

I stood frozen, a million thoughts where racing through my small head. No words came out. Pinch yourself, Came that voice in me. Wake up don't believe all this, it's not real. You're stupid to even think he could be really here saying this to you, your just …Riley. These are your thoughts, not his.
I ignored her and stared up at him.
"Please say something." He said, I could barely hear him.
  "Seth, I umm." He cut me off again.
"Oh forget it, this was a mistake, I should know, you're too smart to fall for me or even like me, I ruin everything and I even hate myself."
Don't hate yourself that hurts me.
 I tried talking again.
"Seth I—"
"I'll leave you alone, forget everything I just said "he turned to go, "SETH NO!" I shouted.
"Will you just let me talk for a freaking second? Let me think."
He glimpsed at me.
 "Just wait a minute, stay here, don't move, I'll be right back."
  I ran into the house, now away maybe I could gather my head and think straight, because I was confused and my head felt as if it were in a million pieces and I had to gather the pieces to put back together. Was this normal? Was this what it felt like when a guy confessed his feelings to a girl?
I pinched my arm hard, nothing. Then I bit down hard, still nothing. I slammed my hand against the wall. Again and again, I felt pain but it must have been all in my head. I glanced towards

the kitchen where the knife set was.

I gave up instead.

I knew what I was going to do. I breathed in deeply and closed my eyes.

"Okay I can do this, it's not even real right." I whispered over and over as I walked to my bedroom and reached my hand under the nightstand. I lifted the board up and grabbed the small book that held my life in it. I felt like I was going to fall over and pass out, my heart pace was uncontrollable and very wrong, my stomach was doing cart wheels. Calm down your pathetic. I took a few more deep breaths and ran back outside. I opened the book looking for the right page. I glanced up to make sure he was still there and this was still happening.

"I'm sorry it's just I really don't know what I'm doing or what to say, I'll just mess it up. So just listen to this."

Then I began to read something I had wrote for him, something I had no idea I had even written. Or I think I did, the dream got blurry and at some points I was just telling him how I felt and why I had not told him.

When I finished it I stared at the page until I forced myself to look up at him.

I hoped he wasn't even there or I had disappeared to dust.

But there he stood and even closer to me then I wanted.

Surprised by his expression, it had completely changed. It was now this serious, eager and anxious look. I couldn't really understand it all that well, it actually creeped me out, but in a good way.

The same way a lion looked before he got his prey, thirsty for it.

"Say something please," I asked just like he had before. If he felt the way I did right now then I just wanted to stab myself for real. I grimaced at the thought. He should never feel like this.

He didn't answer me. I glanced away for a split second and he seemed to yank and pull me to him all too quickly. I hit him with a force and lost my breath again, how many times was that going to happen!

He put his hands on my waist with a fierce look in his eyes, I knew now this was all my imagination. This only happened in dreams. I didn't care.

I reached up to his neck with one hand and grabbed his hair. I just wanted to touch it, to be able to feel his hair, his face. I stayed so far from him but here I was almost a part of him.

His hands on my waist were burning hot. I felt goose bumps all up my body. He no longer kept me waiting in my longing agony. He clutched me tighter so there wasn't a single inch between us, our skin electrifying each other.

He grabbed my face and hastily collided his mouth on mine, his hot breath in me, he was all over.

I felt as if I was going to die of no oxygen but I didn't care, I knew I couldn't even get it. Not here, I would have to be far from here.

I held tighter not wanting this to end, for him to disappear and I be left here alone.

I kissed him back fiercely, we moved in sweet harmony. I took in his drug filled scent.

He suddenly moved back away from me in a teasing way with a

small sly grin. I reached out and my face broke in pain of the sudden distance.

"No don't. "I gasped out.

He moved back still against the fence and I leaped up to him.

He grabbed me again and his back now leaned against the fence, he pulled me up by my legs and I wrapped them around him. He held me with his strong arms.

I had never been this close to anyone and it felt so right, he made me whole. Only he could do that. I didn't want to be happy with anyone else either. I loved him too much, but then she spoke and I was reminded that I had to remember always, this was just a dream...

∞

3. *Angry waters*

I woke up late the next morning, I was slightly more depressed then the usual. I did not want to get up. I had tried repeatedly to fall back into that dream. It did not happen.

I also felt drained, not just of the small joy I had gotten but also some of my dignity. It was great while it lasted, and I had forgotten the chains that held me when I was awake in the world of reality.

But now it was gone, it felt like a thief had come by before I had awakened and ripped out that piece that I had just filled. I swore I could feel the hand markings of the latex gloves pulling at my torso as I began to wake up.

When I did I took a long cold shower, hoping it would get

the feeling off of the hands yanking out what I was holding onto so hard.

I jumped up when the phone rang which made me spill some of my cereal and milk on the table, fruity pebbles to be exact. I growled and ran for the phone.

"Hello." I said bleakly into the mouth piece.

I could hear laughing on the other end, already knowing who it was.

"Hello?" Still more laughing and talking but not to me.

"Hell-o? Come on talk to the person you called!" I sighed annoyed with the thought of just hanging up.

Finally she spoke. "Hey it's me, what are you doing today?"

It was Abby.

"Why?" I asked,

"Just tell me what you're doing!" she said again.

"Why?" I asked again stubbornly.

"Ugh ok that means nothing, well were all going to the beach, just us girls though."

"Were in New York, where are you finding a beach?" I asked her as she got distracted on the other line once again.

"Oh yea it will be a long drive but it will be fun. Riley I am not asking you to come, you're going!"

I rolled my eyes and thought stay at home and mope and probably think too much or go to the beach with my idiot friends? I thought of the stress both would cause.

"Okay, I'll go, what time?"

"In an hour or so". She replied as I heard her jumping up and down telling Kay I was going too, and of course Kay screams through the phone.

I held the phone away from my ear and yelled.

"Grow up you dorks! I'll just walk over when I'm ready."

"Yay, Adios!" She blurted out before hanging up.

"You're not even Spanish!" I said one last time laughing.

I heard her giggling as the phone went silent.

She's so stupid I thought to myself with a giggle. I finished my cereal and changed into a white tank top and jean shorts and pulled my hair into a high ponytail and then ran out the door before my thoughts could consume me anymore.

This would be good, my mind will be distracted and I had not been to a beach in a long time so it would be fun. Yeah I said it, fun.

*

The waves crashed over the sand, I admired how they never stopped creating waves. I listened to the pelicans that made loud disturbing sounds in the air, but it seemed to fit with the ocean just right.

I looked out onto the ocean for as long as I could before getting distracted, it was hypnotizing. The sun slowly moved down almost touching the tip of the water.

It was beautiful. But also kind of eerie, the ocean never seemed to have an end, it just kept going. It was fascinating to think about.

I was disappointed with myself. I should have known that coming here would not help. It just made me think more.

I can't ever make it go away.

The beauty of the scenery just screamed Seth, anything that had a hint of beauty in it, or sadness or mystery. Was him. The color of the ocean was like a pool of his eyes, I wanted to dive into it and never come out. I couldn't do that, I was terrified of the ocean water and what was underneath. Just like how I feared being so close to him, it could only hurt me.

The smell was soothing. I sat on the sand, picking at it and tossing it through my fingers.

The wind was strong and my hair a mess from the salty wind. The drive here was long like Abby had said, but we did have fun, we must have sung along to thirty songs. I snapped out of my illusion and noticed the voices of some familiar people. It was Seth, Vince, Sean, and Michael.

Of course they would find us. I waved to them but did not get up from my spot. I don't know why; I think I was praying I would disappear again. I heard Seth tell them he was going to go say hi to me first.

Nope I'm still here. I thought.

My stomach tightened hard and my breathing got raspier.

"Hey Rie!" He said with his ruggedly sweet voice coming closer to me. I ignored the feelings passing through me because I was truly excited to see him. I wished he would sit here with me the whole night, but I knew with his friends here that was not going to happen.

"Hi." Was all I replied in a weak gentle tone, he gave me a quick nudge and he asked if I wanted to eat with them?

"No thanks I already did, now I'm just enjoying this view."

"Sweet, I'll see you later then". He smiled showing his teeth. I nodded and he ran off.

I watched him and the goofballs run over to the food table and laughed as they fought over the food.

Kay and Abby had walked off to find a restroom. Vince was trying to find someone to go with him to look for an ice-cream machine, he had gone on for about fifteen minutes about how much he wanted ice-cream. It was kind of funny.

I looked back to the clear sea, this time my view was blocked by three young men with surfboards. I watched them for just a minute or two, they were pretty good and they made it look easy.

Paige and Sonny jumped up from behind me. I thought of how I kind of liked being alone, even though I hate my own company.

"Let's go ask those guys if they'll let us try." Sonny said to me and Paige. I gave her my concerned look. "We don't know them Sonny, and it is not smart." I peered up at her eager face.

Paige now on Sonny's side tried to convince me. "Come on, have a little fun!"

"No way, this is how trouble starts."

I saw their going with or without me faces now.

"Ugh I swear I'm like your mother, fine but I'm only going to watch you guys and stand at the shore!"

I got up slowly considering it still, and went as they dragged me to the shore.

I looked back to see the guys still laughing in their own little world.

"Hey can we try?" Shouted Sonny. I flashed her with a warning. She already had her flirty get up on.

I looked at the strangers. One wore shades with short blonde hair. The other two were a little older, one with long blonde hair and the other was dark-haired with huge dimples.

All three immediately walked over with wide grins. I rolled my eyes. I already knew this was a bad idea. Sonny skipped to the younger looking one and began her game of innocent flirt.

The other blonde gestured for Paige to come to him, and of course she went with a huge smile on.

The dark-haired one stared at me stupidly I shook my head no and was just about ready to go find my spot again on the beach when he started talking to me.

"No really, I wouldn't get on one of those things even if I were paid, no thanks"

"Oh well you should at least know how to work it just in

case one day you want to."

He cut me off again, "then you can think of me when you're a pro at it"

I crinkled my forehead in confusion.

"Yeah, still no." I replied.

He was now closer.

"Look all you do is put your hand here"… I wasn't paying much attention to his words. I looked over him at my friends.

He babbled on and showed me about two times how to hold the board.

"So you want to try?"

"No." I replied. I noticed he was now too close to me, my cautious radar buzzed its limit. And right when I was about to say something he slid his hairy hand down my back.

I yanked away and backed up.

"I said NO." I gave him a nasty glare.

He stood back shocked, offended and not sure what to do next.

That's when I noticed Paige; the long haired guy had pulled her to his chest.

She gasped and screamed at him.

That's when I lost it. I was furious now and uncontrollable. I grabbed the board and leaped at the blonde that wrestled with her and hit him in the back of the head with a strong force, he fell back and let her go.

I shouted in anger. Then I gasped a cry when the dark-

haired guy came up behind me and groped at my top.
I tried to punch him but he stopped me.

Right as I started screaming in frustration, he was
yanked away from me by familiar olive-skinned arms.
Seth jumped in front of me.
He threw a hard punch in the dark-haired guy's direction
and he fell back a little, he was angry and shocked but was
having trouble standing straight. He muttered something as
the blonde I had pathetically struck, ignored Seth and tried
to grab at me. That's when I looked at Seth. His eyes were on
fire. He had the look of an enraged killer as he pounced on
him and began beating him, a lot I could tell from his
adrenaline rush.

Both the young blonde and Sonny stood there in
extreme shock.
The hairy guy started to move in to help his friend, that's
when Sean ran at him before he could touch Seth and
tackled him.
Oh that bastard is trying to hurt Seth!
The voice in my head screamed full of rage.
Michael grabbed me by the arm before I could move, which
made me full of more anger.
"Stop them now Michael!" I screeched trying to free my
arm, I didn't want anyone touching me right now.
He nodded with such confidence which confused me for a
moment, than he reached into the back of his jeans and to
my bewildered surprise so swiftly took out a small handgun.

My eyes opened wide, I could barely hear him shout with the waves crashing down behind us, but it helped, everyone froze at the sound of the gun shot in the air. I jumped as Sonny screamed at the sound. It was much more deafening then one would have imagined.

I watched the gun and I watched Seth, if it even aimed slightly towards him I would seriously go into a hysteria attack.

Then Michael spoke, his usually soft and caring voice now held a deep violent tone full of power.

I barely heard his last sentence to them. My cell phone in hand about to call for help.

"Get out of here assholes!" He said aiming the gun like he had done this before.

I was even more surprised when they gathered themselves and took off. Sean had to hold Seth back for a minute.

Whatever he said must have really scared them off, most guys didn't ever give up.

I ran to Seth.

"Are you okay?" I asked already knowing he wasn't. I wanted to touch his face.

"I'm fine!" He yelled in anger. I flinched back.

"Son of a bitch, who did he think he was? I'm sorry Riley, you just have no idea how pissed I am right now".

"Mikey put that thing away now!" I ordered him.

With a grin he slid it back into his jeans. Sean had Paige by his side and was concerned but also upset about the gun. They walked off arguing with each other under their breath. I didn't take my eyes off of Seth. "Calm down, it is okay relax, breathe." He kept his eyes on the guys who were almost out of sight now.

"Relax, they're gone." It took him countless seconds before calming down to a normal human madness.

He stopped shaking but he still had his fists clenched tight to his sides; to the point where they were turning white over the bone.

I knew I would regret it later but I grabbed his hands and gently opened his fists and filled it with my hand. My heartbeat quickened, I felt the ripping in my stomach and the dangerous heat coming from his hands.

I thought of my rule, the one where I measured the times we ever touched. I could barely even hug him, I got stiff and my brain turned to mush.

When I did hug him, I did no longer then three seconds; even though that's how most hugs worked. I was paranoid and always had my urge of wanting to keep holding onto him.

If not I would overwhelm myself and be stupidly depressed all day thinking about it.

Right now I was not thinking of myself but only of him, and even though I knew I wasn't making him feel better, I felt I had to try.

I watched him slowly relax, and I forced a smile.

45

"Better?" I asked.

"No." he muttered.

Being close to him even for a few seconds made me feel like a match to a candle, I wondered if my face was red. Sure that was heroic and it gave me butterflies but I was only worried about him and how angry he was.

Seeing him like that upset me, whatever his mood was, it was mine too.

"That was a pretty hot blow there Riley." Michael pointed out as he tried to calm Sonny down, she wasn't used to her flirty fun going wrong.

I snapped my head at him with a glare.

"Okay, too soon." He added.

"What the hell did we miss?" Whined Kay coming towards me with Abby.

Sonny still full of surprise rushed over to them to explain.

"Let's go, I'm sick of the beach." Seth said firmly his eyes here with us, I could recognize their softness again.

"I couldn't agree more." I said, releasing my hand from his grip desperate to remove the heat he was causing.

He gazed at me with his smile that vanished my revulsion right away.

"You probably shouldn't have seen me like that. That was another side of me, it kind of took over me." Seth said as we stood at my doorstep.

46

"Oh trust me it's fine, you know you didn't have to do that though. That choice could have got you hurt, or in trouble." He looked at me with his shock and confused expression; I liked it a lot, it made me smile and I forgot what I had even said.

"What the hell kind of line is that?" He asked still using that expression. I stared like a retard.

Pay attention!

I found my words again, and repeated myself.

"You did not have to do that."

"Yes I did." He continued, "I got to show off how sexy I look when I fight and no one messes with my Riley, you're one of my true friends you know. And there hard to come by, there was no choice to make." He said play punching me in the arm.

"Ha ha, well I'm honored Seth." I said sad that his expression was gone and now all that lingered was his good-bye face.

I thought he would just turn and walk off but instead I saw he was going to give me a hug first.

Don't you dare, you've done enough for today.

It's just a hug, I thought and why not I had ruined myself for today already.

I breathed in deeply and embraced his strong arms. He smelled like the ocean but under that I could still make out his intoxicating scent.

As he walked away I felt him take something with him. The

same way he did every time... it was my heart.

∞

4. Black rose & a grave

We stood under the moonlight sky and gazed out onto the ocean and watched the diamonds bounce off the water, the moons reflection and shadow were breathtaking. We listened to every wave and heartbeat.

The sky was a perfect blue, just like your perfect eyes; though sometimes they appeared green at night.
The wind was strong and my hair kept falling in my face. I watched you as swiftly as you reached into yor pocket and pulled out and handed me something I had never seen before.
A beautiful black rose. I held the delicate flower in my hand and felt the thorns on my skin.
I did not smell it like they did in those cheesy love movies, but I did hold it too tight to where one of the thorns stuck me, we both

laughed.

When the blood had started to appear I quickly put my finger in my mouth, which made you chuckle again. I tasted the metallic flavor of blood and swallowed it quickly.

Seth admired that, how I did not act like a normal girl and laugh and think he was corny or act all mushy and jump up and down crying because I got a stupid flower. You liked seeing in my eyes how excited I was to have gotten such a strange flower that was black and not red, pink, white or yellow.

You said I was unique for stabbing the thorn into my skin instead. I just thought it was me being a klutz.

You pulled my finger out of my mouth and teased me not to cry. I whined that I wouldn't cry I just did not want blood on my black rose.

You lifted my finger that no longer bled and made me gasp in surprise when you stuck my finger in your mouth.

"Eww!" I had gasped playfully, but I got serious quickly because you were was so intent.

You let my hand go and smiled.

"My magic saliva has healed you my love."

You said with you sarcastic tone.

"Yes it has." I replied without looking at my finger.

Then you spoke again switching to your serious voice, I thought it was funny how you kept changing you expression and tone.

"This is for you and I'm going to tell you why a black rose like this seems so right for you. A rose like this, black, symbolizes sadness and pain, and when I look deep into your eyes, behind that smile, I see just that. At first I was confused because you're always so happy when you're with me. And that's when I realized its only when were apart that that pain in your eyes is so clear to me."

"So this I give to you to symbolize the pain not just you feel but we feel when we're apart, we don't need a red one to show how much we love each other, or a white one to show pureness. We have this black one to show us how strong our love is that when were apart, we hurt."

After you spoke the wind had gotten stronger, almost trying to blow me away from where I stood.

You reached up and brushed my cheek as you pushed the hair away; I did not even realize you were wiping a wetness away from my eyes that had been waiting just over the edge of my eyelids. I did not want to cry, I never did and I felt weak to have almost cried.

You spoke again. "I'm so sorry I have put you through pain Riley, it's my fault and I hate myself for it."

"Hey." I whispered to you.

"Don't you dare blame yourself for my pain, it was my choice and I would never change it. I'm okay really."

"I should have noticed, so many times you said you were fine, and you seemed to be hiding something, but I never guessed it was about me. Your mouth spoke a lie, but your eyes told a whole other story of hidden truth that I should have seen."

Your eyes reddened in sadness and this time I couldn't help it, I had never seen you cry, and it hurt me to see it. I was glad I had never seen you cry before, I don't think I could have bared it.

It wasn't pleasant and I was grateful men barely ever got that emotional, because it's so honest when they do. It really got to me and seeing him like that made it hard to breathe.

I wanted to hug you desperately now and make you laugh or do something to make you smile again.

But I couldn't control what happened here, this was just a dream. But even so, my imagination and mind knew what to do. So I held on to you with everything I had. When I did that everything went wrong, you didn't hold me back; and the waves got so strong they were only a few feet away now. The wind began to circle us like a tornado.

The rose I still held in my hand around you back had suddenly begun to burn but I did not let go, and then it disintegrated into dust.

Right before everything went black a big wave swooped down on top of us and we were gone…

"Shh, you're going to wake them! Paige screeched in a whisper.
"It is okay babe, you're fine and if any of them try to get you don't worry, you'll be the first to go." Sean teased.
"Oh come on dude you would scream and run like a little girl." Vince said stomping on the dirt.
"Stop it!" She screamed louder this time.
"Shut up you guys! I'm trying to listen." I looked at them as we kept walking along the path in the graveyard.
"Listen for what?" Paige asked me bewildered.

"To the spirits, duh." I replied smiling, she was so naïve.

"Oh ha you go on and laugh now but when the zombies come out and kill you, you won't be!"

I rolled my eyes.

"Well yea I'll be begging them to take me with them not screaming and running like you, and just so you know they do go for the loudest ones first, I would.

I wouldn't want to wake from the silence of my tomb and have to deal with a screaming idiot; I would definitely eat her brains first."

She froze and scanned me with her eyes.

"You're so mean Riley!"

"Oh relax you don't really believe the dead will wake and kill us all, unless maybe Kay was here with her loud mouth. I would rise from my grave just to kill her."

"No, but it's still creepy here." She replied a little more calm.

"Well of course it could happen, I just plan on befriending them not being their meal." I continued enjoying her torment.

Paige grilled me.

"Oh I forgot you like this stuff, you weirdo."

"Hey it's always the brave fascinated ones that make it out and live, sometimes even with a depressed sexy vampire." Her eyes lit up,

"Oh nice."

"I think this conversation is draining me of life." Vince said grossed out by my last sentence.

"Come on Sean can we go now?"

Paige asked him still panicky.

Sean smiled. "Oh I wouldn't be so sure Riley, do you know where the meaning of 'Saved by the bell,' came from?

"No." I lied, this would be good. I thought.

"Well I heard this story long ago of this disease that passed through some states and a lot of people were presumed dead from it.

Later they had decided to recycle caskets because they were running out of space to bury people and when they opened up the caskets they found scratch marks and teeth marks on the inside walls of the coffins.

Some bodies were even turned over with their backs to the coffin lids.

Which scared so many people that they had an idea of tying string on the wrist or ankle of the body, then they would thread it through the coffin and up through the ground, and at the top of the grave they mounted a miniature bell tower, so if you ever were buried alive and woke up you just ring the be-"

"SHUT UP!!!" Fear was all over Paige's face.

"Isn't that awesome! And it's a true story!" I said amazed by the story once again.

Paige scowled. She really was spooked now.

"Boo!"

I turned around. Seth had come up behind me and tried to scare me.

"Seriously Seth? You of all people should know I don't scare easily."

He frowned. "I know, but it was worth a try."

I smiled. "Wow it's really humid out here." I stated to anyone who was listening.

"Yeah tell me about it, I'm sweating over here." Sean replied.

After a few minutes of walking down the path all of a sudden Paige gasped and jumped back pointing towards a bench a little up the path. Sitting upon the bench was a little old man with his dog. The man sat there so still you would think he was dead. Paige now in a mini hysteria attack started screaming dramatically under her breath.

"Calm down Paige it's just a little old man!"

"No umm I think it really is time to go now! Sean, come now!"

I started to take a step towards the man when Vince grabbed my arm.

"What are you doing? I know you like looking in the night for vampires but I think you should leave the old man alone."

"I want to go make sure he's ok, it's late why would he be out here alone?" Sean looked at me with an irritated expression.

I glance at Seth. He sighed. "You guys should know that nothing would stop her from walking over there and investigating. Come on Riley."

I smiled, ha he's on my side.

Stop smiling so much.

He gestured and we started walking over to the old man.

I heard Vince mutter something under his breath as we walked away.

Paige was pulling at Sean's shirt to leave but I could see he was curious too. The man looked in his mid -seventies, but he seemed healthy. As we came closer the dog sat up.

I took a step towards him but Seth pulled me back, I chuckled, so protective... I loved it.

"Hey excuse me sir, are you okay?"

We both waited, he still had not even looked at us; he was just gazing out into the graveyard.

"Hello?"

"Hello?" Seth asked waving his hand in the air.

"Okay that's weird, come on." Seth whispered to me.

We both turned to walk away but the dog got up from where he sat and began trotting over to us. Seth immediately stopped in front of me to protect me. I smiled and then got serious. "Oh calm down Seth he's not going to eat us."

The dog then began pacing back and forth from us to his owner.

"What's the matter baby?" I asked the dog.

Seth was about to grab me and walk away but then the old man started talking.

We both froze and listened.

"I loved her, I really loved her, more than anything in the world." He was talking so slow and still had not even glanced at us. His eyes locked on the graves.

We both stood confused, but I could tell this man just wanted to tell his story to someone.

"What the hell is he talking about?" Seth whispered to me.

"Shh, wait." I whispered back.

The dog now walked over to his owner and sat back down with his head resting on the old man's lap, he quietly whimpered as the strange man began to tell his story…

"I was sitting in an old fancy restaurant in Tokyo, I was alone and minding my own business enjoying my meal. Then there was that moment my eyes set upon her. She was beautiful, delicate and majestic. Her long hair pulled into a huge braid and her deep brown eyes showed sadness. She sat with another man. He wore a black hat and suit.

They were arguing in another language. I watched them get louder, I looked around but no one else seemed to notice there heated conversation; though I could tell she did not want to fight, she seemed sick and tired.

I learned her name was Wenny and his Shane. I watched her get up to leave but he yanked her back down. She said something else and then tried to leave once again but he would not let her, that's when I felt obligated to interfere; I did not want to see her upset, and the man had made me angry now. I thought it was strange that I felt strongly for her when I did not even know her, but I wanted to know her.
I jumped up and made him let her go,

I shouted, maybe too loud and this time people actually noticed. He ended up getting upset and just left. I offered Wenny a ride home and from that day on we fell in love.
I had now believed in love at first sight, I never did before. Wenny changed that. She changed a lot. Changed the way I thought about everything, and I was happy.
…It had been a year later and we were staying at a hotel in

Chicago. I had planned to propose to my dear Wenny that night.

We were unpacking our things when all of a sudden two men barged in yelling in Chinese and waving guns in the air, I understood some that time. I knew exactly who the man with the hat was, I knew by the look on my beloved Wenny's face, I had not seen that fear in her face since the day we met in that restaurant. It all happened so fast, Shane hollered to the other man whom was pointing his gun at her and I knew if I moved toward her he would shoot.

He grabbed her then, I was already trying to get to her but Shane yelled and pointed his gun at me.
She screamed and begged him not to hurt me in her language, he shouted back distracted by her.
I then jumped on him and we struggled. I tried to get the gun from him but instead it went off. The other man let go of Wenny and ran. Shane froze, he was shocked but I could tell he really didn't care. That's the moment my life was destroyed.
My heart blew into dust. I looked to see the love of my life limp on the floor. I ran to her though I knew it would not help…"

I stood closer to Seth wincing at the pain in the old man's voice. He still would not look at us.
"It happened so fast but it plays in a horrifying slow motion every single day. Love is rare and powerful."
"Don't waste time, every second counts, you won't know if the last time you see someone really will be the last time ever."

"So…" Seth asked "If she were still alive, would you still be together?"

The man finally looked our way and I was confused by why Seth had just asked that. Of course they would be together. The man did not say another word, he turned away again and stood up walking to a grave, he gazed at it then rested his hand on the gray stone and then walked away vanishing like a ghost in the night.

∞

5. Consuming thoughts

I chose a table hidden in the far back and sat down by myself, trying to block everyone out in the loud cafeteria. I had not touched my food, just sat there and stared down at my sprite bottle. I watched the fizz bubbles move around the plastic.

Some went up, some went down and some fizz bubbles even stuck together. I stared for a long time, even as I reached for my iPod and stuck the earplugs in my ears. I really liked the song that played first, it had such a nice melody to it, the girl sang with so much depth. It really expressed how I felt sometimes when I woke from a dream and scanned the ceiling. A pain started rising in me and I quickly switched to another.

This one was a loud rock song, I turned the volume up high, after sometime I began to realize something. The screaming in my ears actually helped me block my mind from thinking so much.

I closed my eyes and followed the lyrics to the song and tried to make myself seem free through the song. And of course right when I was beginning to trail off somewhere else, free of my minds captivity, it vanished and my mind started up again, my heart shattered over again, my stomach felt the sharp heavy metal beam weigh me down. It felt harder to breathe once again.

I opened my eyes in pain to see who the culprit was that had ripped my earplugs out. I saw brown hair and glasses sitting down at my so called hidden table.

"Hey, I found her!" She squealed out with her French accent. I put the iPod away knowing it wouldn't do me any good now.

"Don't ever rip my earplugs out of my ears Paige, are you crazy?" I said scolding her. She laughed. I looked over her shoulder and saw Seth, Vince and Michael talking in a corner where she had called too. I got excited at first, seeing Seth raised high spirits in me. Then I pushed my lunch tray away.

"What's wrong? It doesn't look like you've touched your food." She asked curiously.

"Not really hungry." I said back in a lie.

I could not eat now, not with my emotions and hormones

going insane. I never really was able to make myself eat if I knew he was so close.

Sometimes even if I'm alone, it really depends on how I'm letting my mind control me at the time. I hated it but I even had to hum to myself and really distract myself just to eat. Most of the time I got to finish but sometimes I got to nauseas.

"So I was thinking …we should all go on a camping trip, what do you think?" She looked at me fixing her glasses.

"Hey that's actually not a bad idea that sounds fun, let's do it!" I replied as I watched her toss my sprite bottle back and forth in her hands.

It made the fizz bubbles go crazy. I crossed my arms against my chest.

"Maybe next week?" I asked her.

"Yes!" She replied as she got up tossing the bottle to me and walked away.

I flashed my eyes down at the poor little fizz bubbles now calm as I stood the bottle up straight.

I decided to spend the rest of the lunch hour observing the cafeteria. At least everyone I could see from where I was. I saw a couple at a table making out.

Next to them were some guys eating and listening to music. They seemed really bored, one was sleeping with his head resting on a book.

I looked back at the couple, he was now laying his head on her lap and she played with his face. She grabbed a napkin and stuck it over his face as she giggled and he whispered to her.

They whispered and did pointless random things with each other, I thought it was pretty pathetic, I laughed at myself as I was thinking. They were so stupid, but at the same time I knew. I knew I would do the same little things with Seth, acting like a teenage couple and all lovey dovey, if I could.

I hated that he made me feel like that, made me want to act that way. I was not someone who participated in the whole thing, none of it at all. I just seemed to never fit in or even wanted to. I was a loner in my own world and that's how I liked it. I preferred to just observe everything. I came to realize over time that Seth changed that for me, he made me want something so much that I never cared for before.

I looked away to another table because my mind was trailing off again. I knew that by the pain in my chest. The next table was empty. I stopped and started searching for familiar faces.

My eyes landed on Vince, I spotted him hiding behind the snack machine, and he was eyeing Sonny while she sat chatting with some girls. I could only see part of him from where I sat so I had no idea what he was doing. I looked around for the other guys and saw Sean and Michael were sneaking up behind Paige, Abby and Kay. I smiled searching for Seth, what were these guys up to? I got up and started to slowly move out of there way when I heard someone behind me.

Oh crap, I thought.

I turned and was immediately soaked with water in the face. I gasped in surprise and started laughing. "Michael what are you doing?" I cried out.

At that moment everyone was running around the cafeteria and screaming as the guys with water guns chased everyone around.

I stood wiping the water off my chest while Michael laughed, then he stopped.

"My bad Riley, maybe I shouldn't have done that, are you ok?"

He looked remorse and upset with himself.

I laughed because he was so weak, he couldn't even stick to his own joke.

"I'm fine, go!"

He ran off laughing again and shooting water everywhere.

Sonny came running behind me and stood in my shadow trying to protect herself.

"Sonny no don't!"

I called out as she blocked herself with me.

Everyone was so loud! Where were the professors and security?

Seth came chasing her with a big orange gun and huge

smile, he stopped right in front of me. I gazed at him with an innocent smile though I couldn't breathe again.

He mouthed for me to move and I jumped out of the way and he soaked her down. She squealed in shock.

"Riley you traitor!"

"Ha as if I'm going to protect you! Yeah right."

She growled and ran to the bathroom.

I rolled my eyes. Abby and Kay came over to me both drenched in water and laughing hysterically.

"Come on Riley!"

They pulled me to the exit and we ran out into the parking lot, we got in Kay's car and she drove off.

"Wow everyone better get out of there or there's going to be huge trouble." Kay said aloud.

I put my seatbelt on and grabbed my cell phone out of my jeans when it vibrated.

Seth -   Hey, where'd you go?

Riley -   lol umm out of there. I don't want to get kicked out of college. Oh thankz 4 not shooting me :)

Seth -   Of course I would never, I actually like you out of the whole stupid school :P And don't worry we had it planned, no one will know what we did.

Riley - Aww, well that made it all very mature lol

Seth - I know right, can I b any more mature? I so don't act like a kid anymore :D

Riley -   Haha, your awesome Seth.

Seth -   I know =P

I closed my mouth and looked around, I was smiling way too much. I let out a sigh of annoyance and slipped it back in my jeans.
      "Where are we going?" I asked.
They both were still laughing and telling each other their version of how they got attacked.
"I'm hungry." Abby said eyeing a burger joint.
 "Oh me too!" Kay added.
 I was starving, maybe I could eat some fries without feeling sick. I stared at the car carpet and spaced out and thought to myself. Why I did get so worked up over a simple conversation like that? I really was pathetic to be like this.
      I took a deep breath and stared out the window. I watched everything pass by, the cars, people, buildings, street signs and trees.
I watched the clouds in the sky move slowly.
"Riley!"
"Oh what I'm here, I'll have fries and a water."
"So," I asked. "What are we doing now?"

"Well, I got to go to work so we will eat real quickly and then you guys can drop me off and then go study. I'll study tonight when I get home." Abby informed me.

"Ok, where do you want to study Kay?"

"Your place!" she replied fast.

"Ok hurry and drive off, the worker there is staring at us like were crazy, especially with how soaked we are." Abby laughed and Kay screamed out the window.

"Kay stop! And drive!"

I peered out the window and stared at the sky again hoping for another text message to come, but none came.

*

"I HATE MATH!" I screamed into my pillow.

"Okay let's take a break before you kill someone." Kay said closing her book. I looked up from my pillow.

"Yessss!" I said singing it.

She reached for the remote and turned on the T.V. "What do you want to watch? And please none of that mystery forensic/murder stuff."

I frowned at what she said and began to speak but she cut me off. "No superhero stuff either."

I rolled my eyes and gave her a response I knew she could not refuse.

How about reruns of that old show we use to watch.

"Now that I can agree on!" She replied eagerly scanning the channels. "Yesss! Here we gooo! She stretched her words as she found the show I was thinking about, funny how she knew what I was talking about.

The doorbell rang and I jumped up when Jack started barking aggressively.

"Geez, relax Jack you give me a freaking heart attack every time!" I got up and slowly walked to the door, maybe if I walked slowly they would just leave. I looked through the peep hole.

"A pizza man?"

"Yes!" I heard the muffled voice from the couch.

"Kayleen! We just ate not too long ago!"

"But I'm hungry again! The voice from the couch replied with a silly child tone.

I sighed and opened the door. "Hi." I muttered grabbing the box from him. He gave me a huge smile that annoyed me.

"Kay come pay for your food!" I looked back at him, the look on his face made me weirdly uncomfortable.

"Woah your eyes are sweet are they contacts?"

I smiled a fake smile hiding my irritation.

"No their my real color." I replied.

Kay ran over to where I stood at the door with her money.

"Ok bye." I said closing the door.

"Nice apartment-" he blurted out before I shut the door.

I threw the box on the table and flopped back down to watch my favorite actor on the screen make a joke.

"Want some?" Kay asked with her plate in my face.

I glanced at it shaking my head and pushing it away, "Fine, more for me." I rolled my eyes. "You know I saw that." She said again before taking a big bite out of her greasy slice of pizza.

"Why do you have to be so mean and defensive towards every man you pass?" she asked chewing her pizza loudly.

I felt a lump in my throat. "Because there all stupid and every guy I meet I just don't like the bad vibe I get from them."

"Because you never give them a chance to get to know you, you know maybe start a little something." She now laid down on the couch still chewing, with her legs in the air swaying them.

I replied again. "Well maybe because I don't want to, I'm perfectly fine single."

"No you're not." She said eyeing me. "You may not want any of the guys you've met, but you want something, and you would be a perfect wife."

I snapped my head over at her surprised. "A wife?" I asked.

My eyes opened wider as she chuckled.

"Yes from my observation that's what you are."

"What observation? You can't observe nothing longer

than a few seconds." She squinted her eyes at me.

"Ok so Kay your saying I'm that girl the guy settles down with in the end and starts a family and all that?" She smiled big now. "Yup I hate to break it to you but you're not girlfriend material, you Riley wait and don't search your whole life for guys. You will just have that one serious relationship, and whoever he is he will be so lucky to have you, especially with that big passion in you and the way you talk."

It took me awhile to take all she said in. I ended up replying with a simple laugh but I knew she was right, but I wasn't sure if what she said was good or bad, knowing my situation.

"And he was right about your eyes and home, it always smells so good here, I love it and it's so..."

"Homey?" I said.

"Yes very homey!"

I looked around my home, with burgundy walls that bear black and white pictures I had taken of nature and old Christmas lights that I could not get myself to take down.

I laid on my red love seat and she now sat bouncing on one of the black bean bags. My carpet floor was a fluffy white and I had candles placed through-out the room.

I thought aloud to myself. "Today is Thursday, I'm going to the library tomorrow."

"You're going to school on the day we don't have to?"

Kay asked.

"Well I got nothing better to do and I can't actually look for books when you guys are all there. I have to go into a zone when picking them out."

"Whatever, I'm going to go to a water park with my baby."

Her baby is her boyfriend Tacom.

"Cool." I said as my stomach growled. I glanced at the pizza again with the same ending decision I had before.

*

I skimmed over book after book. I had just returned my last six books last week so I was fresh out. I walked slowly through every aisle. I did not want to miss a book. Soon enough my pile went from three books to seven and I finally finished with a total of thirteen books. This should last me awhile. I thought and laughed at myself.

I stacked the thick chapter books high and picked them up walking now to the staircase, barely able to see where I was going.

I was on the third floor of the library so I had to walk down a lot of stairs. These were made in a spiral, a long twirl of steps. I looked down over the books and the bar. Students were either at computers or quietly studying in their own private cubicle.

I started down the stairs slowly holding all the books in front of me.

I passed the second floor and as I walked I couldn't help but lose my concentration. My mind wondered to Seth, somehow making my stomach spin just like the stairs at that moment. I went blank as I took the next step. I tripped and went lunging forward on the stairs, my books flying everywhere; some over the rail and down the spiral steps, others around me as I rolled down the last few steps and made it to the ground.

I heard gasps and someone howled. I looked up now dizzy. One of the books had hit a guy in the head. I stumbled to get up in shock.

I was on my knees now. I couldn't help myself but I started laughing, I wanted to say something or apologize but I couldn't get it out. I was having a pathetic laughing attack.

Some students drew their attention to me looking concerned, others were trying not to laugh. I slowed my laughing,

"Oh great Riley, just great!"

I heard a voice playfully say behind me.

It never mattered what he was saying, his voice was just like an angel, so soothing.

Musical voice box, that's what Seth had. I turned on my knees feeling like a complete fool. My arm hurt but I didn't care, it was all too funny; of course Seth would be there somehow.

I kept replaying my fall in my head.

"Wow." It was all I was able to get out. I laughed more.

"What the hell did you fall for now?" he asked looking down at me.

Falling for you. I replied in my head laughing again.

I stopped and frowned.

"Oh no the books!" I muttered as I crawled over and started picking them up to start my pile again.

"You just fell down stairs and could have broken your neck and all your worried about are the books?" I stopped and gazed up at his glistening eyes and big smile. I knew that meant I was smiling now too, but a joyful smile, different then my usual.

"Yup." I replied.

I swear if my life depended on it I could never look at him and not smile back when he did, especially when he also used his eyes.

I quickly turned away. If I stared back to long I would go numb and either hot or cold depending on the look. I slowly got up looking away. I felt the tenseness in my body creep over. I looked at everyone staring at me. I mouthed that I was okay. Seth grabbed the rest of my books and helped me carry them to the check out. Then he walked off and I watched him till he was out of sight, I breathed out realizing I wasn't before.

"Ugh I'm so tired!" Kay mumbled half asleep.

"I'm hungry." Abby added. Everyone stared at her. We all knew she was always hungry.

The clock ticked on by slowly as it always did at this time. We were waiting for Benson in our English class. "Monday's are always the worst, after three days of sleeping in, it's horrible." Paige said with her head on her desk. I looked around at everyone. There was a chick with blue hair a couple of rows down staring at the clock. A few guys were talking to each other in the back row. And two sisters whispered back and forth next to me. Besides the group of friends I hung out with everyone else I realized I did not really know.

"Sorry I'm late class, accident on the road." The professor said as she rushed in and set her things down. Everyone stopped talking.

"Okay." she said.

"Today we are going to do something different. I want you all in a circle."

A few of the students moaned. "Are you serious this is college not preschool?" Vince said snickering. She gave him the not-in-the-mood look.

"Let's just do it guys." I said getting up and dragging my chair to start a form.

She waited as we all moved like turtles to make the circle of chairs. She was wearing a checkered long sleeve

74

shirt with jeans and a thick black belt with boots. She looked tired and stressed though she tried to hide it with her smile, but I could see right through it.

Minutes later as we were all sitting in the circle. I noticed the chair on my right was empty. I regretted it before I let it happen but I had no control over my mind, it controlled me. I pictured Seth sitting in it and smiling at me.

I immediately shook my head and peered down.

No. No. Stop it Riley!

Benson started talking but I wasn't really paying attention, which I hated. I wanted to hear her but I was now fighting illusions in my head once again.

Then I looked up, someone had come in late and sat in the chair next to me. A small burst of air made me suck my breath in as an intoxicating scent blew my way. *Damn it!*

I looked over and he glanced at me with a smile.

He was wearing a black t-shirt and blue jeans. I wore a black sweater and also blue jeans. I guess we kind of matched. I thought. But I wasn't focusing on that, even though it was my favorite look for most people.

I watched him intently as he slowly ran his hand through his hair. His muscles flexed and veins bulged when he moved. My heart pounded against my ribs.

I fidgeted nervously with my sweater.

I was having my own personal episode, a psychotic

impulse to touch him. He was just inches away. I wasn't sure what was making me like this at the moment but I didn't like it one bit.

Why was I freakishly enticed by his arms? And fascinated by the veins I could see through his soft olive skin?

I put my hand in a fist and pulled the sleeve over my hand and forced myself to look away. He was driving me crazy and he was just sitting there.

The thoughts were getting stronger and the images were taking over my whole view. I closed my eyes and took a deep breath. It was cut up and forceful.

I was getting mad now. It was winning and taking complete control. I just wanted the urge and pain in my chest to leave me alone.

That's when I noticed the pain in my hand. I opened my eyes and looked at my arm, and it was slightly trembling. I grabbed it with my other hand and stopped it.

I released my fist in pain, the fingers slowly got feeling and I stared at my palm. My nails had dug in pretty deep. I examined the small red crescents I had made. I noticed Vince looking at me and sighed hiding my hand again. I screamed at myself a little while longer and finally was able to be in control and I could hear Benson talk again.

***

Journal Entry 106

There just dreams. If they're supposed to be here, don't let them consume me, if there poison to me, take them away...

***

∞

6. Beauty in the dark

I did not want to sleep, it was almost two AM and I was tired but I just didn't want to. A lot was racing through my head that I couldn't concentrate on trying to sleep. I sat up in my bed and scanned my room, there had to be something I could do better than staring at the ceiling all night.

I decided on music, it seemed to help me in ways not explainable. I climbed out of bed and walked over to my dresser and picked up my iPod. I stuck the headphones in my ears and selected some rock music and turned the volume up high. I crawled back into bed and laid there staring up until I finally drifted off…

I was no longer home in bed, I was now somewhere dark and cold. There was a thick fog in the air and I was freezing. I looked down and noticed I was dressed in a tank top and short blue jeans.

My hair was straight and down, not in the mess of a bun I had made before I had laid down in bed. I shivered and rubbed my arms up and down. Why was it so cold here? It was a dream, right?

My eyes were trying to adjust as I realized my surroundings, the walls were made of a dark clumpy stone and closed in around me, I thought about what this place felt like and I realized I was in a cave. I started getting up from my knees when all of a sudden I noticed something cold brushed the tip of my arm as I slowly stood, I almost gasped as I realized there were bodies around me, at least ten.

Dead bodies I assumed, they laid with black coats on, and some I could tell were woman. One had gold curls hanging out from under the coat.

I didn't scream, though I wanted to. I didn't know where to escape, it was so dark I could only see around me and there was no distant light that would suggest an exit.

I wondered to myself why it didn't smell bad, it actually smelled good here. A sweet kind of aroma filled the cold cave, but I was too confused to think about it so much.

I started walking aimlessly one way. I just had to get away from these dead bodies. I couldn't see the ground beneath me but I didn't step on any bodies which was a relief.

I had passed them and made it to a rocky area, but then of course my boot bumped into a pebble making a crackling noise in the cave. What really irritated me was the loud echo sound that followed.

I stopped in my position when I suddenly got a chill and knew there was something behind me. Something was lurking right around me, I felt the eyes burning through my back.

I don't know how but I heard them now. Alive. I heard the sounds of hissing, like a snake but raspier, more deadly. So loud that it felt as if it was coming from just an inch from my ears. I slowly turned to see them standing there, staring right at me, all so still. I was so confused. They had looked so dead a moment ago. I stared back my eyes widening. I just stood there, as if some stronger power was not letting me move my body or eyes, it also made me not want to even move. I had never felt a power over me like this unless I was in the presence of him.

Then someone – something spoke.

"What is this?" the voice of a man said followed by more hissing. I kept silent, my eyes still not in full focus.

"Why it's a woman Skye." Whispered the one I noticed before with hair so curly and very yellow, almost as if strands of bright gold itself.

"Yes." He said with a tone that suggested he was smiling. "I can see that thank you for pointing it out Cynthia."

His voice was deep and serious like one from a God.

I could not stop staring in his direction. Though I could barely see, suddenly I wanted to see his face, to see if his face matched his intriguing voice.

"A beautiful woman actually."

She smirked. I got fidgety and shivered again.

"And what might be your name?

"…Riley." I blurted out in a whisper, surprised by the strong firmness in my own voice. Though I felt like I was shaking.

"Ah Riley, that's a peculiar name." He said.

I moved my shoulders trying to make out a shrug, it seemed I was only trying to keep myself standing instead. This whole situation was just strange.

"So how may I ask did you come upon our home? It's not such a safe place here dear." He slowly walked forward pulling the hood down from his face.

My head spun, his face was pale white with purple and red depth around his eyes. The eyes were a silky red, his lips also with the same color, but as if they were bruised. His skin was tough and smooth, perfect over the bones.

His hair a golden brown, it was a terrifying sight but at the same time, it was like looking upon an angel. A dark angel of night, and in some strange way he seemed so familiar but I couldn't put my finger on it.

I was now getting very irritated, I didn't like that I was so mesmerized by his face. I didn't even know him. I wanted to just run away now.

The only man I ever thought was so beautiful was my Seth. I mean Seth. He wasn't mine. I felt the spell or trance that seemed to be compelling me at the moment. It was making me so angry even though I didn't show it.

I tried not to look at his eyes because something told me evil was beneath them.

I knew he was doing something to me. I kept calm though, I had to be. I couldn't flip out and scream like an idiot. I knew it would do

81

no good because I knew what he was.

I knew exactly what was happening, this was a horror scene seen many times on television. I usually enjoyed it and I could picture myself in the story, but not this way.
I was stuck in a cave with vampires. This was not the irresistible immortal that falls for the human girl thing. The look on his face was anything but welcoming.

"So ironic don't you think, it must be destiny, for this beautiful woman to appear at this time." He grinned a wicked smile. I finally broke out of my daze and looked around to see the glowing eyes of the, I assumed vampires.

That's when I noticed something else, a body on the floor. One that had not magically come to life; drained of blood with a terror stricken expression on what looked like had been a man.

Dead white with eyes that were stony and colorless, I jumped back a little and made a muffling noise as I knew my guess was right. The blonde Cynthia noticed and giggled, then she moved towards me real fast, in a split second she was inches from my face.
"Are you scared?" She asked.
"No. ...yea, maybe a little." I replied.

She was taken aback with a shocked look on her face, must have expected me to freak out or cry.
Though she could probably hear how fast my heart was beating.
"Can I kill her already Skye? I'm getting bored." She asked him aloud.
I made a mental note to myself, don't get a female vampire mad.

I looked at him again to see what his response would be.

"No."

He said shifting his gaze to me again. No?

I was shocked at that, with his eyes on me and mine on his, he spoke again.

"Go, all of you, I will take care of her."

"But, why--" he cut her off by raising a hand.

"That's an order Cynthia."

She hissed with spite and fleeted out of sight along with the other cloaked vampires following behind her.

I turned back around to see he was closer to me, too close, more then I wanted him or anyone to ever be, but something kept me from running.

It must have been those eyes; the instant I looked not even with all my power could I break away from the stare.

I knew exactly what was going to happen, I knew almost everything about vampires and mythical creatures, vampires had always fascinated me. There was so much that appealed to me, the whole tortured soul, dark and mysterious thing.

I just never thought I would ever have a deadly encounter with one. A human and blood thirsty vampire, in his dominion, alone. I swallowed hard fidgeting in my spot. Realizing that was not such a good idea to do in front of him. It seemed he had released his old expression and now had one just filled with some sort of lust.

I watched him as he stared at my neck, probably following the blood flow in the veins. I wasn't afraid; this would be a sweet quick death, as long as I didn't fight it. It would not hurt at all. I knew

there was no escape or any way to defend myself either.
After exasperating seconds of our weird and uncomfortable stare down.

He lunged himself toward me to close the long gap between us, making me gasp I threw my hands up automatically and closed my eyes. He yanked my hair pulling it away from my neck. With his other hand on my waist squeezing very tight, I winced in pain. I was breathing fast hollow breathes now. I just stared up to his confusing beauty, I did not care even though I knew I was probably about to die.

With an eager lustful look on his face he leaned into my face and inhaled deeply. He moaned and hissed in my ear.
"You smell better than any woman I have drunk from, but then again I have never decided to savor one so much." His hand was cold on my waist even through my top.

This is just a dream, I thought. It's just a dream. This will all go away soon and he will disappear.
As if he knew what I was thinking, I felt him pull my top up and slide his hand under. I trembled and shivered from the cold. He seemed to like that too. I felt the anger in me build. I was going to die anyway but he was too close to me now.

I did not want him touching me, even if it was a dream. I tried pushing him away but he did not even seem to notice.
I wanted to scream in frustration, but I could not.
It seemed he had control over everything except my thoughts. It was riveting.
I noticed his building pleasure which build my hate more.

84

I felt the thrust as he suddenly forced me against the clumpy dark wall of the cave, his hands held tightly onto my arms. I gritted my teeth and grunted in anger.

Could he not just do it already!

Before I could say something he surprised me by jamming his dark bruised mouth to mine, his cold lips were hard. I tried pushing more.

It didn't make sense to me. Vampires never did this. They never cared for kissing or felt any kind of joy from it. That was a human thing. All they wanted was blood.

I felt a raging fire in me, I was completely useless and had no control.

He was holding me so hard that I could not move at all, but I was not hurt either. He had the perfect hold. I continued to try and push him away with my arms, but it just made it worse. He wasn't supposed to do this!

Just bite me, I thought.

After a few seconds went by I gave up, he was just too strong for me.

He forced his tongue into my mouth, making it even harder to breathe. I grumbled trying to effortlessly pull away. Then I tried by reaching up and yanking on his hair but all it did was entice him more. I let my arms fall to my side. He finally pulled away and grabbed my neck with his hands.

He pulled the straps of my tank top down so that I was bare for him to suck me dry. He smiled shining his pearly white teeth at me making sure I saw his sharp fangs appear. He grabbed the back of

85

my neck and exposed my neck wide and plunged his mouth into his desired spot.

I jolted at first, his sharp teeth punctured my skin like long needles.

It hurt so much but I forced myself to stand still, the pain then reduced. Now I just felt the pressure of the blood surging through my veins. My vision was slowly fading, I felt colder now and empty somehow. I felt dizzy, numb and I started slipping down the wall, my legs had gave in, but he held onto me not letting me fall. I felt weak now, but then something weird happened, it suddenly stopped.

I looked over to see him frozen in his stance, I felt the terror build on my face and I forced myself to scream.
"What are you doing? Finish me already!"
His fangs retracted and he just stared at me. I could see sadness in his dark red eyes.

"Please finish!" I looked down to see the trail of blood down my chest. I moaned and tried to reach to it but I was so weak.
I forced myself to reach again but he stopped me and pushed my hand away. He gripped tightly on my neck with his whole hand to stop the blood from spilling out. I cried out in pain.

"Please!" I whispered panting. I grabbed onto his arm trying to yank it away. I had lost too much blood, I was weak and he was stronger now that he had taken in more blood.
"I'm sorry, I can't." He said with no expression on his face.
"I can't just let you die cold, colorless and empty."

"Why? You do it all the time!" I asked still in shock.

"I don't know, but I just can't." He was speaking slowly.

I watched him reach into his pocket and take out a knife, still holding me up with his other hand, he brought it to his wrist and made a small cut, the blood oozed out and I tried to move my face away.

"What are you doing?" I pleaded.

"Shut up and just drink it!" I froze as I felt the panic build at the thought of being forced to drink blood.

"Umm no! I'm not doing that! No! No!"

He stared at me more and then forced his wrist into my mouth. The warm blood started filling my mouth, I tried not to gag, and his wrist was covering my mouth so hard. I could barely breathe with all the struggling I was doing. It came to the point where I knew I had to just start swallowing it.

I whimpered in agony and the painful burning from the bite on my neck. The blood tasted like rust and after a while turned into a strong cherry taste. I knew it was the only way to stop it all. So I drank.

Slowly I felt feeling come back to me, and color filled my face again. There was a sudden burst of strength in me as well. This time I was able to rip his arm away, I touched my neck but it was smooth. The bites were gone.

"No! No! No! This is not supposed to happen this way!"

He looked scared now.

"But I saved you."

I pushed him back away from me. He flew back pretty far to my

87

own surprise.

I dropped to my knees and held onto the ground, now all I felt was a mixture of hate, and somehow compassion for him and then suddenly there was a loud snap and everything went black...

I woke up late and drenched in sweat, I sat up slowly and looked around, but I couldn't think, my thoughts were all being drowned out. I ripped the headphones that were still blaring music out of my ears and crawled out of bed. I stood in front of the dresser mirror, light shined in through the window. I leaned in and examined my throat, nothing.
I checked my teeth, no blood or anything, they were just how they were supposed to be. I breathed in deeply. That was a relief... I started off my day with a long shower and brushed my teeth repeatedly.
What was I thinking? It was a dream. Though I was curious to the slight disappointment I felt from waking from the dream.

∞

7. Precious Fire

I got home as soon as school finished, it was the same of course. I played my music to try and drown out my thoughts. I tried to avoid useless conversations with my friends. I was disappointed not to see Seth in school, I hated when he skipped.

Every day seemed the same, unless something happened that actually made me feel more pathetic then I did about myself.

At home I scanned my bookshelf till I grabbed one of the books I had gotten last week, when I had my great memorable fall down the spiral steps.

I was about to open it when my laptop beeped, I glared over at it for a few seconds then got up and picked up the smooth silver square object. Just some notifications on social media.

I scanned over the recent post of my friends, and then I did something stupid. What was I some crazy person? *Yes.* I regretted it every time, I knew I should not do it but I could not help it. I don't know why though, it just hurts. I clicked on the small square picture of Seth, the page loaded to his profile. My chest felt heavy, the uncomfortable feeling came over me. I growled at myself. I should just click the logout button and continue reading the book that laid now abandoned on the coffee table.

But instead I clicked on all the pictures that were posted all over his page, like a virus or bug infestation, the pictures swarmed his profile. My eyes felt heavy when I clicked on a picture of him holding her. I was sick to my stomach, when I had no right to be. Now that made me click the button I should have just moments ago before seeing these pictures. I felt the pressure still building in my throat. I forced a deep breath and threw the laptop far away from me.
I was angry at myself.
I violently grabbed the book and went to another room, this room felt infected right now. I let out a sigh of disappointment.

I remember swearing to myself I would <u>never</u> be those woman that let a man be there everything, and without even realizing it, I had…I had failed.

I hated myself for that… not loving him, I could never hate loving him, it was the only part of me that felt something real. That nothing compared to. Life had not been able to steal that from me. Nothing could poison it, but the consuming of my mind I did not like, that was stupid of me.

*

"So Paige, my best friend, can I get some?" Kay asked sitting down next to her with a fake, funny expression. "Please, please!" She added batting her eyes in Paige's face. Paige laughed passing her the bag of chocolate. I listened to my friends joke with each other as we sat around the circle we had made of either tree stumps or baggage.

I could not take my eyes off the blazing fire in front of me. The smell of burning wood and the cold night made it so relaxing. I was in my own little heaven. The moon was bright in the dark sky and trees surrounded us.

I held a marshmallow stick in my hand watching it slowly burn. The fire was just breathtaking.
The flames were high and I listened carefully to the crackling noises it made in the air. I could sit in this silence forever.
I loved it so much because I felt like I could relate to the fire.
I had that fire, right inside me. I could feel it burning.
Rising higher every moment.
Then I also could see Seth as the fire, something so beautiful and powerful. I felt drawn to it by just the radiating flames, but I just could not touch it…

91

I could not concentrate on it that much though, there was the nagging feeling in me that felt like a growing knot in the pit of my stomach.

He was just a few feet away.

Sonny sat close to him with her stupid smile on. She kept grabbing onto his arm and giggling at her own stupidity.

What was she 14? But who am I to think that, I should not be picturing myself pulling her by the hair to get away from him. He seemed to like the attention from the leech on his arm anyway.

What guy would not like it?

I was so out of it I did not even realize I had burned the marshmallow to a charcoal black.

I wasn't even going to eat it anyway.

I glanced over at my friends for a quick moment. Kay had chocolate smeared all over her mouth and she was laughing with a hysterical crazed look. I couldn't help laughing. She looked like a dog with rabies. Abby was sticking her eleventh s'more in her mouth as she moaned at how good they were.

"Oh nice you're wasting perfectly good marshmallows Riley!"

Kay said with her eyes wide and big smile of smeared chocolate.

"You want to eat it?" I asked.

"No."

"Then shut up!"

She smiled and then took it from me, she smelled it and made a grossed out face.

"I dare you."

She glanced at me pretending it looked fine now.

"Sure it looks yummy." She said before sticking it in her mouth, just a second later spitting it out on the floor and coughing.

Everyone laughed.

I stared back at the fire. Then got startled as Abby jumped up excitedly with the biggest smile she could get off her small face. "You guys I have a great idea!" She announced so enthusiastic with her hands in the air it was even annoying to me.

She looked like a kid when offered candy. Everyone turned their heads to look at her.

"Let's play manhunt!"

"Yeah!" Kay added jumping up too.

"Come on let's make teams." Vince agreed.

"Aw man but we don't have glow sticks, they make it perfect." Kay noted disappointed. I put my stick down and walked over to my tent and grabbed the bags I had stashed in my back pack and with a grin tossed them to her.

She squealed with joy.

"Riley you're the best!" She jumped for countless seconds then tackled me with a bear hug.

"Calm down geez, get off me! I knew you would end up wanting to play and forget them. Get off!" I repeated, you are going to wake the wild animals!" she stopped and got off me.

"Oh, or the Vampires!" Paige said excited with an eerie smile. At the sound of that word I instantly whipped my head in her direction. "Umm no, no ok now go play guys have fun, enjoy." I said fast as I sat back down around the fire. "You're not going to play?" Michael asked looking at me concerned. I loved when he was so sensitive.

"Do I ever? Nope, I'm good right here." I replied picking up the marshmallow stick again and adding a fresh one. I let out a loud sigh so they would get the hint and leave, I really didn't want to leave the fire. They took about ten minutes to leave since they added jokes in every thirty seconds. My friends were crazy, and then they were gone.

I closed my eyes and listened to the crickets and the wind. What was I doing? Only couples did this sappy romantic stuff, and here I was alone, in the wilderness, by a fire, listening to the stupid bugs and wind. It felt like just a few minutes had gone by when I heard a twig snap. I opened my eyes looking up. Of course, I thought.

"Hey, you got tagged out already?" I asked.

"Yeah," he replied, sitting down beside me.

I caught my breath, I was annoyed that the whole night so far all I wanted was for him to talk to me, sit by me, smile at me, it's all my stupid head did. I flinched a little slowly moving away unnoticeably.

"Hey! Having fun?" He whispered giving me a punch in the arm I barely felt.

"Yes sir," I replied looking up into his eyes, the fires reflection in them brightened up the night somehow.
It made me mad.

His power affected me so strongly it seemed inhumane. My heart spluttered hyperactively and I sighed letting out a deep gust of oxygen. Not realizing I did it out loud like before.

"What's wrong?" his for head creased and he showed me his doctor expression.

"Nothing, I'm fine." I replied smiling. I already knew he was going to notice the fakeness.

He then gave me the, I-know-your-lying-look.

Though for some dumb reason I did want him to somehow see I was sad, I brushed it off and said I really was fine.

"What about you?" I asked a little more depressed now that the pain had doubled. I caught the hint he was hiding something too. I felt a screw drill through my chest when I saw it or thought it.

"Just...Stuff."

"Stuff, really?" I retorted. "Seth! You can tell me anything. Good or Bad, I don't care how dumb you think it is, I want to know." I brought my shoulders down.

Stop being so dramatic! I thought.

He looked up at me with a fake smile, it made me sad. I couldn't make it go away.

"I just …I don't know, not in a good mood I guess, the smallest things irritate me. Nothing ever seems to go my way." I glimpsed at him painfully, I knew how that felt, and I wanted to steal the pain and thoughts away from him.

"I'm sorry." I whispered. I didn't know what else to say, there wasn't much I could.

I watched him slowly move his hands through the fire, he looked to be enjoying it.

"Careful," I blurted halfway reaching my hand out. I stopped midair bringing it back. He chuckled taking a stick and waving it towards me.

"Ahh, don't hurt me!" I laughed. He stopped and pointed at the stick in my hand.

"Me? Look at you!" The third marshmallow had burnt to crisp and the end of the stick was on fire.

"Give me," he said reaching for it.

"No, no." I said tapping it against the dirt. He glared at me. I was still bothered he hadn't told me what was wrong.

"Shh, did you hear that?" He paused.

We both froze and listened, and once again the night was filled with a long howl.

"That's awesome!" I said overly loud and excited. We heard it again a few times and just listened.

"She sounds so sad but yet it's beautiful. Seth did you know wolves don't howl at just full moons? That's a myth, they'll howl any night and mostly during the twilight hours."

He gave me a curious expression that made me pause.

"What?" I asked.

He smiled, "You said, she, how would you know that?"

"I don't know. I just do."

"Are you guessing?"

"No." I replied. "

I just know it's a female by the sound of her howl, she's crying."

He gave me a look as if he thought I was crazy and it made me laugh.

"Do you know why they howl?"

"Tell me what you know Rie," he replied returning the curious expression. I liked it.

"Well, a wolf's howl can last up to eleven seconds long and there's different reasons and howls behind them. Howling helps the pack communicate in huge areas. It also helps to call pack members to certain locations. Or of course they'll howl to protect their territory. Howling is also a way they can tell which particular wolf it is. Kind of like how fingerprints work for humans. The coolest thing is no two wolves will howl on the same note. There's a harmony, even if they start out on the same note, one will change their tone in the end of the howl. No one really knows why but some believe it is because it makes the pack sound bigger and threatening to intruders. Wolves mostly just enjoy howling though, kind of like people and singing. Then there's the lonely howl, which is heard mostly in mating season when the wolf is searching for their mate. Isn't that beautiful?"

I looked up at Seth.

He had on that look that made me think I was talking way too much. I felt a little stupid now, my excitement sometimes ran wild.

"Riley you find a lot of things beautiful."

"Yeah I know sometimes too much." I replied.

"No that's good." He said smiling.

Make up your mind. I swear you're the king of mixed signals!

"So how much of that did you know already?"

"Most of it," he replied grinning.

"I just wanted to know how much you knew."

"It's freezing!" Abby squealed.

"I loved it! That was so much fun!" She added skipping towards us.

Moment over.

Paige was cleaning her glasses while she leaned against Sean's chest. I felt that weird faint tug in my gut. Which made me feel overwhelmed with a sense of holding in my breath to long, but I was only holding in words. I could live through that.

It was time for me to get away. I stood up trying to ignore the annoying emotions going threw me too quickly. "It's late, let's go to bed." Sonny said yawning.

I pushed the pain away.

"No bed. Tent remember, nice hard floor." I corrected her.

"Ha! For you guys." Kay said across the bonfire already in front of her tent and trying to pull out a single sized portable blow up bed.

"Wow." A few of us harmonized.

I turned back to Seth and in a whisper said goodnight, it came out awkwardly. The expression on his face was very different. I had never seen it before, it was very light.

"Night." He said. I wished so badly to have the ability to read his mind at that moment. I would want to know what he was thinking every second of the day.

He reached in for a hug, something people did everyday very easily but of course I felt so much, I hated to have to think it over so much too. I hugged him tight and tried to concentrate on my three second rule.

It felt like the part in a movie where everything is in slow motion and the intensity is fogging the air up. The crowd is just waiting and holding their breath. His hand moved slowly away, too slow. Almost as if he were lightly brushing his hand against my shoulder as he pulled away. He glided his hand from my back to shoulder. It was torturing… and it meant nothing.

He still had the same unreadable expression on and it made me crave more. He slowly moved away keeping his eyes locked on mine, the look in his eyes made me want to smile really hard. I liked it, it made me feel numb and I felt like I had taken a sharp breath in.

Then Seth just turned and walked away.
I knew I was crazy and it was all in my head. It had to be.

I got to my tent really fast and zipped it up, I was relieved I didn't have to share a tent and that I had one of my own. I sat on the hard floor with my blanket. I found myself taking deep breaths and running my hands through my hair.
I stopped myself. Was I a crazy person, or overly dramatic. I did not know.
I was invisible to everyone and my mask was down, I felt it leave.

My mind kept on racing. I didn't want to think about it but I had just felt slightly like a vampire, in those moments of controlling their animalistic nature and not giving in to their mortal love and robbing them of their precious blood. I knew what the power of resisting felt like.
I erased the thought out of my mind even though I knew it was true. I was happy and calm. All I had to do was think of that smile and the way those eyes could look at me.
It gave me the answer to my absurd way of thinking and living. It was all worth it if I could just see those penetrating eyes and beautiful smile. I could lose just that so easily, and I knew I could never let that happen.

*

I woke up early before anyone and got myself presentable before leaving the tent. I sat on the stump from last night. All that was left were some ashes and smoke. And since the fire had burned out it was cold, but I liked that too.

I sat with my book and read for a while, moments later of complete boredom and rereading the same lines over and over I started making sandwiches for the group. I couldn't stop myself from glancing over at Seth's tent and trying to think of a funny girly excuse to wake him up to be with me. Maybe I thought I heard a bear or I needed him to do something for me...No. That would be pathetic...

As I finished preparing the last one, I heard the laughing mixed with screaming coming from the tent on the far left. The tent opened, to the sight of a few crazed looking girls that really needed a mirror, they looked like they had just rolled around in the woods. I smiled under my breath.

"Good morning Rie, oh food!" Kay blurted with a huge smile reaching for the plate in my hand.

"Hey um where's Seth?" I asked sounding as if I really didn't care. I was really good.

"Oh he left." She replied with food in her mouth. I ignored the pain I knew would come and shrugged. Vince appeared and picked up a sandwich without the plate and stuffed almost half of it in his mouth. He nodded his head starting to speak.

"It's expected Riley."

"Yea I know." I replied. "Well now there's an extra sandwich."

"Yes!" Kay shouted coming out of her tent and grabbing two plates and then sitting down. I thought to myself, oh what precious moments I had... It never felt enough. But, it had to be.

The rest of the day was ok, I mean good. It wasn't great though. Nothing was unless he was here. I hated to be over powered, but that's how it was. I did have fun with my friends, don't get me wrong. I always did. I laughed real hard when Abby got us lost after reading a sign wrong on the nature trail, she most of the time read everything wrong and was clueless but we still loved her. Well I did anyway. Kay got all freaked out and ran to me wanting to hold my hand, she was such a baby... Or the time when they both wanted to go fishing but no one else wanted too. They went anyway as the rest of us watched them saying how dumb they looked trying. Ooh and the best part when Kay was trying to help Abby put bait on her stick when a squirrel came out of nowhere and snatched it, making Kay furious and made her automatically start chasing it, screaming along the way that she was going to kill it. Abby cried out to leave it alone because it had to eat, and the rest of us were just laughing are butts off.

Kay had grabbed a tree branch and started for it. The squirrel turned on her and started chasing her back and now she was terrified and running for her dear life. We all paid attention then, rooting for the little rodent. We did have fun, we always did. Weird, but fun… it was just different when he was around even though he made me so tense and cautious, I was happy with him and that's what counted. The rest of that day, Kay swore revenge on that squirrel.

I did have a good time, even though he made a somehow grand thing about his presence. He had no idea. I knew his smile was a huge part of that… If he smiled, you did, known fact.
I've heard so many people say.
"A guy is never worth it". But they didn't know Seth, or at least not like I did, I saw him differently, and he was worth anything…

We were now on our way back to the city in Mike's car, Vince had taken everyone else with him.
"Oh let's stop for fast food! I'm hungry." Abby randomly said still with the ear plugs in her ears.
"Okay!" Mike agreed instantly, what guy didn't want food. He whistled under his breath as he pulled into a fast food sub place. We listened to her order her food that took over 5 minutes.

"Would you like a drink?" The robot box asked. I think it was a man.

"What do you have?"

Mike and Abby listened to the robot recite the list of drinks they served there.

I'm not sure why they asked, the list on the menu was right there.

I pointed it out to them but the guy in the box still listed them, I repeated them as I heard.

Diet coke, coke, sprite, dr. pepper, orange soda…"

"Do you have iced tea?" She asked the box.

My mind had vanished and I was now thinking about his favorite drink that was just said, the knots in my stomach begun.

I tried ignoring it right away but then that picture popped into my view. The picture I saw online, it was nagging at my stomach real bad. Mostly because I was shocked, I had expected a super gorgeous girl, but she was not, she actually seemed ugly to me and others around me. I think it was just the raging jealousy and pain.

I hated that. I guess he found her attractive, and I know it's not about looks, I knew that for a fact, it is what's inside that matters. That's what bugged me so much.

Of course, it made me think he really liked her for more than that. It would have helped if she were beautiful and looked like a snobby girl that went through many men, but she seemed innocent and probably nice to.

Could she deserve him?

Probably.

No.

I think not a soul deserved him, not me either.

 No one.

The pain came harder.

I couldn't push it away this time.

"Want something Riley? Mike asked.

"No." I replied bleakly looking out the window.

I tried distracting myself with the cars that passed by, the
tall buildings that were coming into view, people who
walked on the streets, the green trees and even the blue sky,
but nothing really helped…

∞

8.   Plain Horror

I was frozen.

Literally.

As if time had stopped. Everyone and everything had become still all around me. The cars that usually sped by were all still and silent. A woman across the street stood still by the bus with her phone to her ear, no movement at all.

There was no wind in the air, the trees didn't sway back and forth and the leaves didn't fall to the floor. The sky was a steel metal gray, no birds or planes moved. The clouds were not even moving at the slow speed they usually did.

I was about twenty feet standing from a little car. It was parked in front of me, and the sight of the car made me want to move, but I couldn't.

I was suddenly afraid of what could happen.

I wasn't sure if maybe my hearing was messed up, I had never walked outside to not hear one car or person. It was just too weird.

The only thing I could hear was my heartbeat and breathing, which was already at abnormal speeds.
It got even worse as I stared at the cars color knowing it was so familiar. Anxiety rose in my stomach. This small blue car had aged. It seemed now like a car you would find in a junk yard, but when I had last seen it, it was sleek and shiny clean.

Then I saw a movement, I blinked and looked around. It was coming from inside the car, I tried to move, but I was still stuck. My breathing got heavier and I watched to find the cause of the movement. The passenger door slowly opened making an old creaky noise, like a rusty door to an abandoned house.
A middle-aged woman stepped out of the car. Something seemed familiar about her too but I didn't know what. I was desperate to move a muscle but could only see. She walked with a smile on her boney face to the back door of the car. She went in and pulled out a small little boy.

He was beautiful. Maybe two years old, I couldn't see him that clearly, but just the slight features I could see were breathtaking. The baby boy was angelic and almost unreal. The woman stood by the car with a smile as she held the boy to her.
I was confused.
What was going on?

Who was this woman, and the little angel she held.
I wanted to hold him, but I remembered I couldn't move.

She hollered at someone inside the car, there was someone else now.
I could hear her. My hearing was fine, but other than the commotion around the car everything stayed still and silent, as well as me.
I watched as patiently as possible and focused on the woman, the baby boy and the door that was slowly opening on the driver's side of the car.

What I saw then sent a pain right in my direction. It hit me like a gust of wind. I felt like a nail that had just been hammered into cement.
The pain was different, it made me cold, numb. I felt dead. It was what I imagined death would feel like. The figure that walked out was Seth, handsome and manly. I couldn't see any more youth in him. I watched him walk over to the woman and her baby. I was struck by pain everywhere. I saw him reach for the baby to hold as I took in the same jet black hair and the blue eyes that shined between them.

My stomach cracked with horror, I felt a burning in my chest and I started to hyperventilate. I wanted to run, I wanted to close my eyes and run away like a kid, but I was stuck. I was stuck in a hell I never wanted to be in. I was forced to watch the happy family in front of me. I couldn't even move my face away. The pain *made me want to scream.*

I felt empty,
like a field without flowers,
a sky without stars,
and a Christmas tree without lights,

And Seth.
Well he only had to be one flower, one star, one light. That's all I wanted.

When would it all end and disappear to black?
My eyes began to swell up and my face turned red and I held it in for countless seconds. My insides were swelling with...jealousy. I couldn't even breathe anymore. I wished the wind would blow by. I was gagging and I felt the metal copper taste in my mouth. My stomach lurched and I almost threw up.

I wasn't even trying to control myself any longer.
I was out of my mind, but maybe it was a good thing, maybe I would go so crazy I wouldn't care anymore.
I felt myself crying, something I never did. There was nothing I could do.
I tried desperately to move my arms but it just hurt.

Everything was starting to go blurry and loud around me. Shaking, the whole earth did. A loud screeching noise filled my ears.
The family stood there still taunting me. Then too slowly it all went black, and I welcomed the blindness...

My eyes flashed open, I blinked quickly and I sat up for a moment. My eyeballs hurt, like I had just failed at a two-hour staring contest. I was back to reality. I felt the trembling in me but I was able to control myself.

I got up and checked the time, only three AM. I had to go back to sleep. It was just a nightmare.
 I got up and started pacing back and forth. It was actually relieving to be able to walk.
The pain was worse to think about now awake, I really felt it. In my nightmares I didn't feel the pain as physically, but now it was no longer just psychological.

This pain was different, not like the other pains I would feel. There was the pain of loving him so much. I loved him too much, sometimes I felt it was overlapping my heart. There was the pain of not being loved back in return, but I know other people have felt that.

There was the pain of wanting to make someone happy, but not being able too, or the pain of just thinking of him.
This pain was one of the worst. This pain held no hope at all. I lied back down and shut my eyes, they had burned with the anger I had towards myself. I fell asleep again counting backwards and fell right into another nightmare, even worse than the previous one I had just went through…

At first everything was a colorful mess in front of me,
I couldn't make out anything.
I blinked twice hard and then my scenery came into view. The sky
above me was a dark shade of gray. The clouds were black and
almost alive. They looked as if they could swoop down any second
and take me off this earth.
I had no idea where I was, nothing appeared familiar or right. It
was like I wasn't even on earth.

There was nothing surrounding me, I was standing in an
empty desert, the end of the earth, that's what it felt like. The
ground beneath me was sand. Ok this had to be a desert, but it still
didn't feel normal. There seemed to be no ending or escape, the sun
was like a dying flashlight on the verge of disappearance, the
clouds were gaining speed, they moved fast, too fast. The wind was
pushing me down.

Then I saw something, and I started to walk towards it. A
huge tree was before me. It was the strangest tree, and it was eerie;
it held not one single leaf. The branches looked like a witches long
fingers reaching out to me.
I jumped, startled by the loud smack of thunder. It sent chills down
my spine. I tried covering my ears with my hands, but it didn't
work. The thunder was too loud. I started running backwards
away from the ghostly tree. Then I stopped, not just because I felt a
drop of moisture on my cheek but I heard a muffled scream.

"Is someone there?" I asked looking around bewildered.

I knew I had heard something.

The rain was falling faster now, the thunder deafening me; could it not stop for at least a second! I had to hear!

Than it came again.

"Help!"

A voice pleaded.

I started running again. I knew the voice but I didn't want to think it.

The rain poured down, my hair was sticky and stuck to my neck and for-head.

I skidded to a halt when it got louder and I almost fell over the edge of a surface. Like the end of the world, I looked down to see nothing but a olive skinned hand holding on, I screamed at the top of my lungs in shock.

"SETH!!!"

The edge of the desert was foggy and I couldn't see anything below him, he really was hanging on for his life, if he fell he would...

"Hold on!" I cried out.

I got on my knees and bent over. I held my hand out without looking at him.

This couldn't be happening.

At that moment the flash of lightning let me see his face, I swallowed hard. The panic-stricken look in Seth's eyes was torturing. It made me light headed. I couldn't stand to see any agony in his beautiful face. It killed me inside. My heart pounded against my ribs, I thought of when Ms. Woods would bang on the bathroom door in the orphanage, me and Seth would hide in there and play cards.

"Don't let go!" I shouted as I clutched with all my strength.
I looked into Seth's eyes. "Give me your other hand so I can pull you up!"
"I can't! If I move at all I'm going to fall, you can't save me."
He spoke and was drained of anything that made him Seth.
I bent over more, now almost hanging over myself.
"Don't you dare say that!"
I screamed over the thunder and lightning, I was angry now.
"You don't let go you hear me? Don't you let go! Give me your other hand now!!!"
"No." He replied with a doubtful expression, I hated it.
"If I do that you'll fall too! You can't pull me up I'm too heavy."
I held onto his arm with my life.
"No please, don't just give up." I pleaded, desperately crying, grateful the rain drowned it out.

My arm was beginning to feel like it was being ripped off, but I didn't care. I had to pull him up. He tore his gaze from me and looked down.
"No, No, No. Do not look down Seth."
"I have to go Riley."
He said looking at me again, so lifeless…

"You're not going anywhere, not without me! You promised! Together forever."

"I can't let that happen Riley." My chest throbbed from hanging onto the ledge. My legs felt numb but I had them firmly in the sand. My right arm was beginning to pop from the shoulder. "Damn it Seth! Give me your hand! Don't give up!"
"Riley!" He shouted cutting me off and getting my full attention. "Listen to me, don't you dare jump in after me, I'm telling you not to, do you understand me?"

He demanded loudly with rain falling in his face.
"Yes- But –"
"Shut up Riley."
My mind went blank.
"I love you Seth."
I chocked the words out in a whisper. A faint smile touched his lips.
"I know." He replied through clenched teeth.
"You'll be ok Riley, you'll be ok without me, and you need to let me go."
Then, in a split second he was gone. I felt myself screaming, the pressure had left my body. My hand felt broken. I couldn't feel my arms. My mind was frozen. I felt like someone was using a fork and was yanking out my insides. I thought of jumping in after him, but I couldn't get myself to move. I couldn't bring myself to disobey him and the plea in his eyes…

I woke up numb, sweaty but unmoving. I wasn't breathing hard. I wasn't hyperventilating or screaming anymore. My throat was sore, and even if I wanted to scream, I couldn't. I got up and stood in the middle of my room. Then I walked to the living room like a ghost, I switched the T.V on and sat down.

I felt my face swell up and tears came out, I was crying because I knew how I would feel if he ever left... I couldn't sleep, not with that thought.
I couldn't take anymore.

This was something I was supposed to forbid myself from thinking. This was greater than any pain. Seth not in this world was unbearable to think. As long as he was happy and alive, I could be. The slightest thought of him not on this earth made me sick to my stomach.

Right then my stomach lurched and I ran to the bathroom. I would stay up all night and watch T.V. if I had to. As long as I did not dream.

∞

9. Mourning of Discontent

I sat in my huge bathroom tub and watched the water fall from the spout, it was slowly rising up to my shoulders. I just wanted to be in the water. The bubbles surrounded my body. The voices in my head would not stop. They kept on whispering and shouting things I already knew. Countless scenes of lies and fantasy came to mind.
I sunk deeper in the water. I needed to shut her up, the girl in my head… me.

I felt like two people sometimes, stuck in one body. There was someone in there that hadn't spoken in a long time. She was a part of me that held my heart, the one that feels, hurts and longs. The one that smiles and tells the mind what she wants it to do or say. But I didn't let her. I was the mind to this body, no longer the heart, and the one who decides what to do with it all and how; the one that lied for the best to protect her. I was sad for her. I had taken over her and made her stay trapped, away from feeling.

I went deeper, I could no longer hear anything as the water reached my ears. All I could hear was the beating of my heart and my breathing.
I wanted to drown out the thoughts. She had to shut up for just awhile. The past two years of my life had seemed to get worse with Seth. He really was becoming an obsession.

I went completely under. My heart raced as the pressure in my lungs grew fast. I stayed under for a while, it was shocking to my brain, it told me to go up for air, and I ignored it.
I could barely hear anything now, it was all mixed up. The thoughts had vanished and all I was thinking of was the need to gasp for air. I wondered how long it would take before my heart came to a halt.

The pressure got harder and harder. It was crazy how quickly the body reacted and how weak it was. This wasn't so bad for my conscious. It could take anything, but my body could lose all life in just minutes. It was reaching the point where I couldn't bare it. I slowly could see darkness make its way in my view.
Was I closing my eyes?
I felt I could, I would just give in and die. But I was a coward.

She took control… and then I saw Seth, I felt Seth, I heard Seth and I smelled Seth, and when that image vanished, I found myself jumping up out of the water and gasping for air…

I sat down in my bathrobe on my couch and stared at the wall, since I couldn't shut my mind off, I switched to something else as I felt expressionless in every way. This was starting to consume me.

I thought back to what my youth leader had told me last week. I remembered him looking at each of us in the group. His eyes were fixated on his thoughts. When he reached me I saw a flicker of something. He was talking straight to me, and I was ready and listening.

I also felt guilty; what he was saying, was true.

"All you have to do is let God be in control and you will be content in your heart and mind."

I quoted in my head the words Paul had said.

"It's hard I know, but if you put all your faith in him, in the end it will be great."

I had believed in God my whole life, since I was little. I was always ready to worship or pray when the priest came to the orphanage. I was happy, free- spirited and young, but overtime my faith had weakened. I guess that's what happened when the teen years took over, your life actually started to go wrong. Stress and heartache became a way of life. Your belief in faith and happiness fades.

The pain I felt made me think crazy things. But how could it not? The world was filled with hate and sin. But I did believe in the Bible, it was the only thing that made sense and had pure solid proof. I believed that whatever God wants, is for the best. Pain could easily distract you from your beliefs. Some people would blame God. I thanked him, because I was blessed to know Seth. If I had a chance to start my life over again, I would do it all again and not change a thing.

***

Journal Entry 192

Not a poem or anything special, not something to be liked or bought, just my ~~Stupid~~ thoughts...

<u>"That hidden girl"</u>

As I sleep my mind still consumes me, but no pain I feel. When I open my eyes to the burning sunlight, it comes back over me like poison shooting through my blood, only to reach my heart. This secret side of me is screaming to come out and live, but I won't let her, and she has so much she wants to do and say, but she understands I'm trying to protect her, because if she's released, she'll surely <u>destroy</u> us both. I've created a nightmare within myself and I'm never truly me cause the real me is ~~gone~~ hiding, when this curse came upon me it locked her away.

My mind controls all of me, I'm desperately trying to overcome, but right now I just feel to numb. I smile and laugh like everything's ok. But that's not me. It's the liar trying to keep me together. There's no

119

one to blame but myself and it's up to me to fight this. That's what I'm trying to do. I just want it all to go away.

I could simply let her out but keeping her hidden is also the only thing that keeps her together, My worst fear is that if she ever escapes and does what she's longed for, that the one she loves did not hate her for all my lies.

***

I kept reaching into my tote bag to look at the screen on my phone and then put it away. Did I really think if I kept grabbing it something would pop up on the screen?

I stopped myself around the seventh time when I noticed a guy a couple of rows down was giving me a weird look.

I didn't feel like walking back home from work so I took the city bus, something I did rarely since all the places I went to were so close to my home.

I wanted to smile, a real smile, but only he could make my smile real.

I flashed back to when I was at work and filing papers. I had put my headphones away and worked in silence for hours. My mind had begun to wonder and I was hearing voices. Images were stirring in my mind.

"I love you," came a whisper in the back of my head.

"I just need you to know, even though I'm not what you want, I do love you more then I even should. I'm sorry."

The words repeated in my head. I ended up having to re-input some papers after typing the same thing in over and over. I shook my head and the voices faded.

Shut up!

I seemed to not be able to ignore the phantom illusion of his reactions. Why did my conscious want to tell him so badly!

I heard sweet deluded words, but I knew I was only being deceived. I needed to think reality, where he doesn't speak to me at all, or just shy's away from me with hate. In the end it was useless to think either way. My phone buzzed and I reached for it like it was my inhaler. I cursed at myself. I read the message.

Kay -   Where are you?

Riley -   On the bus, I'll be home soon.

Kay -   Where are you?

Riley -   I said, on the bus.

Kay -   Where are you???

Riley -   KAYLEEN!!!

Kay -   Ha! I love you!

Riley -   What's up?

Kay -   I'm bored and I miss you ☹

Riley -   But I just saw you yesterday.

Kay -   I MISS YOU!

Riley -   Ok ok, then just come over then, if you miss me
                that bad.

Kay -   I'm already here :.>

Riley —   Of course, I'll be there soon ☺

Abby -   Where r u?

Riley -   On the bus, I should be home soon, why?

Abby -   Where r u?

Riley -   -_-

I smiled as I reached my door to find both of them sitting on the steps, arguing over if a cloud shaped either the gates of heaven or a wizard's hat. They both squealed when they saw me and ran over. I always had to think and remember we were in college, not middle school, but it seemed we just never changed.

"Does that look like a wizard's hat?" She asked with a smile,

"Or heaven." She asked real low.

I laughed, "Umm no I think it looks like a bed, and that's exactly what I want."

They both frowned. Kay's curly hair was up in a bun which was unusual. And it looked like Abby had actually brushed her hair.

"What are you two doing here?"

I asked eyeing them as I opened the door.

"Were going to my Aunt's wedding!" One of them replied.

I was relieved and disappointed that I was now not alone.

"Today? Now?" I asked.

"Yup and you're coming if you like it or not." Abby demanded trying to sound threatening.

"No thanks umm, I got to give Jack a bath and you know that could take all night." I replied with a horrible excuse.

She was already heading towards my closet to pick out clothes.

"Wrong one." I said pointing to the right closet.

"That's the pantry."

"I know that." She said laughing at herself. "And you're coming."

She said again now in the right closet flipping hangers real fast. I whined but knew I wasn't going to win.

"Do you own at least one dress?" Kay asked minutes later.

"No. Eww never." I replied disgusted at the thought of me

in a dress.

I checked my phone again.

Dresses had a meaning in them, and I think it's to try and look hot for a guy, and it wasn't something I wanted to do. I don't want people walking up to me and saying oh that dress is so cute, where did you get it. Nope, I don't even want people to glance at me, and heels well I think they were designed by men to make it hard for a girl to run away, I mean really how do you walk in those things?

"Ok this will have to do." She said pulling out a top I didn't even know I owned, it was acceptable, long sleeve dark blue with black floral patterns. "And let's see your heels?"

I laughed to myself.

"What the hell!"

"What, I don't do dresses and heels you know that."

"Oh but you'll dye your hair wacky colors and wear different colored socks and shoes and just look like a plain freak sometimes!"

"Well at least I'm being real and not fake like a lot of other people!"

"True." She said and ran over to give me a hug.

"I love you! I love you!"

I picked out the nicest black pants I had and my black boots.

"Is this good?"

"We have no choice, now get in there." She said shooing me into the bathroom...

*

I couldn't understand the lyrics to the song playing. I wanted to though it was what I was concentrating on the most.
It was a little too loud like every wedding or party I had been dragged to.

The mixture of different colored lights beamed down from somewhere, I tried to find where but ended up giving up.
Everyone seemed super excited. The ceremony was cute, but now I was stuck in the worst part, the reception. I hated this part and not just because I think everyone looked like idiots, I just thought dancing was pointless, or maybe people who were high on life and happy did it. That's cool. But that's not me.

I thought for a while. Yea I would definitely elope to Vegas or something. Just me and him, it's all I would ever want or need. I wasn't a rebel or anything, but these traditions were just fake, in a few years they might be hating each other. How can someone do this three times? I didn't want to be like everyone else, it wouldn't prove that things would be done differently than the world did it.

Unless of course he wanted it, I would do anything he wanted and bare any horror, because it wouldn't matter. I could be with him and ignore everyone else.

I snapped out of my minds useless daydreaming of *ifs* and *ides* and felt a strong wave of sadness.

You won't ever find someone worth it. That you can have...

Everyone was dancing to a popular song, besides my hyper friends, one guy kept staring at me till he had the guts to ask me if I wanted to dance, and he was very persistent. That went real well.

In my mind I cursed. But hey I was nice about it.

Sometimes I just wished people knew how I was.

I got more pissed off minutes after he walked away because he made me think of Seth, and how I wished he was there.

He would have scared the guy off for me. I pictured the scene, and smiled. I wanted to go home, I felt anxiety creeping on; this was too much. Everyone was too happy and everywhere. I felt I didn't belong. Like an ant in the middle of a spiders web. I was always stuck in the wrong place. I only felt right when I was with him, I felt I belonged right there. I remembered the jolt of 100% certainty I would get.

I stared at the phone again and let out a frustrated sigh. I had gave in and texted him. Who knew a stupid text message could mean so much. The thing that drove me even more erratic was when I didn't get a message in return. That happened quite often.

Why did I always try to talk to him? I wasn't important in his life, maybe when we were kids but it is different now. It was like I was halfway through a book, and he was still trying to figure the title out.

I glimpsed around at the pink and white ruffles and string that seemed to cover every part of the reception room. I glanced down at the table, I was sitting alone at it, but that's what I wanted. I looked across the table at the empty chair. I was such a pathetic being.

I started playing with the mints I found in a little tin can with a lacy label, I rolled my eyes, was that necessary. I wondered how much it cost for a little tin can for every single person here, or for the layers of tablecloths on each table, and why the heck did the chair need a dress for? It was a chair. The center piece pretty much took over the whole table. It looked like whom ever put it there spent all day on it. With marbles all around and different random gift objects such as the tin cans and bottles of bubbles. The glass bowl was filled with rocks and water.

"Oh no way!" I sad aloud shocked. Were there live fish in there!

I got closer and watched the poor little goldfish swim around in there, useless and trapped. I touched the bowl to make sure the fish weren't heating up with all the candles lit around it. But it was a really thick glass so they were safe. They were stuck in the middle of this mess. They should be free in a huge area not that little bowl. I decided to mix the marbles around and switched the place cards around. I took the bottles of bubbles and stashed them in my bag. There I thought, nothing is ever really what it is supposed to be, now it was realistic. I smiled an evil smile and threw my bag over my neck and blew out the candle closest to me. I walked into the nearest waiting room, it was quiet and empty just the way I like it. I found a couch and stared at the wall thinking about some homework I had to finish and slowly my vision began to blur.

... *This dream seemed surprisingly okay, and something was familiar about this place. It wasn't like I had been here before. More as if I belonged here.*
I didn't feel any pain at all, and I was not afraid that any would come. I was walking outside a small old house, and the pathway that led to the front door was made of little brown colored stones. There was a long row of bushes that outlined the home and a small little bench in front of the big window. There were wind chimes that hung above the bench, I could hear them chime. There were also birdhouses and bowls of cat food and water placed by the door.

I walked along the front of the house and turned around the corner and was totally shocked to see Seth across the street walking too.

To my own surprise, I ducked and ran. I creeped my way behind the house and ended up in the backyard. I was still confused as to the weird attachment I was feeling towards this little home.

I think he saw me, I thought to myself, but wouldn't I want that?

Maybe it was because I was just a little messed up. My hair was a mess and I wore light blue pajamas. I snuck my way through the yard across some swing sets, a seesaw and a bright silver slide. I saw a big black Labrador lying chained to a little shed and a small grey and white striped cat sitting on a table.

For some strange reason I knew the animals names. The dog's name was Hannah and the cat Cocoa, but how? I had never been here before. How odd! I passed a big tree full of bright red cherries, something lingered on them. I didn't know what though. I had the urge to grab and taste its delicious sour taste but instead I kept running.

I turned the corner of the house, Shoot! There was a gate blocking the way to escape.

What if he had followed me? I tried to fix my hair but there was nothing I could do about the childish clothes I wore. I thought about trying to climb the gate but then I was startled by a voice. "Hey!"

"Oh jeez you scared me, I didn't know you were coming." I said awkwardly.

I felt the butterflies go wild in my stomach.

"I see you have a problem." He stated laughing.

It was as if he knew all that was racing through my mind, I liked the expression on his face. It was so happy and free. It even reached me and I felt it. My nerves were jumpy. He then so quickly jumped and sat on the gate and peered down at me, I looked back with amusement. Then out of nowhere he added,

"Okay I think I will go swimming now!"

He was confusing me so much but it was funny. Then I confused myself as I started babbling off in a bossy worried tone,

"Okay, well you have fun but no sharks, jellyfish or octopuses."

I said counting my fingers. "Be careful." I said pointing my finger at him.

"Well then Riley you might want to kiss me, just in case you know."

I opened my eyes wide.

What?

With the funniest look on his beautiful face he playfully jumped down and walked towards me. I couldn't help but smile and let out a nervous giggle as I stepped back. Was he serious?

I was under the cherry tree now. It smelled so tempting.

"Hey want to see something funny? Come here."

I let him get close this time. He breathed in and I felt his breath in my face. I blinked and my mind went completely blank, how was he doing that to me? He was so evil I thought to myself smiling.

He got closer and closer reaching his arm out, at the exact moment that anyone would have thought he was way to close and about to grab and kiss me. A door swung open from the patio of the house. A lady called out and it made us both freeze.

"Oh my gosh!" I squealed so jumpy and amazed.

"How did you know that would happen?"

I stood dazed in awe.

He had this most lovely smile on his face, I felt so captivated here. He chuckled still staring at me and they just glowed like diamonds on the ocean. I saw a blur of colors and I was gone, everything was black and I heard my name being called...

"Riley, hello what the.-"

I looked around and saw fake plants, chandlers and a big fountain of splashing water. The whole place made of white granite and peach walls. That's when I realized I had fallen asleep on a couch in the hotel lobby.

"Is it time to go?" I asked yawning. I was relieved I had gotten sleep with no nightmare. I couldn't help smiling the whole ride home, even though I was still confused. These were the dreams I loved, even though it was upsetting to end so quickly ...

I stood in front of the mirror after I washed my face and glanced at myself, I had gotten all the makeup off that Kay had forced me to wear. I could see the anxiety, fear and droopiness in my face. I was tired, really tired, but terrified to sleep another night. I had to though, I could. It was just a dream I thought as I got into bed, just a dream, but also the worst nightmares ever…

I was on my knees in a cold dark familiar place. I closed my eyes trying to remember what was going on.
My eyes then snapped open as I remembered what he had done to me. I spun my head towards him, where I had kicked him away surprisingly far, now he was getting up.
I reached to my neck, nothing there. Then to my teeth, nothing either. He hadn't killed me yet, if I didn't die, then I wouldn't turn. The blood had to pass though. I knew this story.

He was walking around and lighting candles and torches making the whole cave brighter. With a disgusted look on my face I pulled the straps from my top back over my shoulders and stood up. This could not be, I was supposed to be dead now, not standing with his blood in my veins knowing if he killed me I would become one of him.
Then from out of nowhere she was there.
The gold curls glowed in the cave.
She was furious.

"Cynthia! Help me!" I cried out to her.

She turned to Skye.

"How could you do this? You were supposed to kill her, we feed not turn our prey!"

He stayed silent, his red eyes and lips in a firm stare.

"Please," I interrupted. "I don't want this, help me." I begged her.

She glanced at me and then back at him. As if I wasn't even there she continued on her rant.

"This is against the rules, you sick tick. I will have to get rid of her myself."

I felt an odd burning sensation in me but I was still human. I ignored it. I had to stay focused.

She started walking towards me but Skye was immediately in front of me, his back against my chest. I got chills but tried to push him away, He struggled to hold me back knowing I was stronger right now with his blood in my system.

She gasped.

"No! Are you serious, what you love it?" She hissed loudly as her fangs appeared.

I stopped pushing him and froze as my eyes spotted something on the back of his neck. At a quick glance I spotted a small tattoo. My eyes grew wide, now it made sense.

Before I could say something I was struck hard in the head when Cynthia lunged at him and he threw me into the wall with his back, I had been crushed and I heard something crack in my head, darkness consumed me…

133

I awoke disoriented and a little nauseated. I noticed I was lying in a bed. I sat up quickly and looked around. The bed was red with silky sheets. The walls of the room were made of bricks and there were candles hanging lit almost everywhere my eyes reached. The place smelled like the same sweet smell, but this time I wanted it. I slowly reached up with my finger and lightly touched my teeth. My finger was stabbed instantly. A rage grew in me. I sucked my finger and wailed out into the air.

I got up off the bed and appeared at the window fast. Wind blew in through the window. I was high off the ground, in a castle or something. I felt as though I could jump twenty-five feet and land without hurting myself. I felt like running fast through a forest. I thought of all these un-human things as the adrenaline rush creeped over.
I looked down to only see grass and trees.
I couldn't see anything else. I was in the middle of nowhere once again.
I felt for my clothes, I was wearing a silky black robe, my tank top and jeans were missing. My undergarments had not been replaced but it made me mad to know someone had been changing my clothes when I was …well I guess dead.

It was cold and I tried to make myself warm but it didn't seem to work. I looked back out the window and gazed up at the stars and the bright moon.
"You've awakened." Came a low soothing flawless voice.
I wasn't startled, I had heard the footsteps coming when I cut my

finger. I turned slowly to see him in the doorway. He had appeared out of somewhere but I couldn't see a door in sight.

"You let me go now!" I screamed trying to release the rage in me. There was a burning in my throat but I ignored it.
"You do this all the time? Turn people into vampires and then kidnap and take them someplace they can't be found!"
"No." He replied in a calm voice.
"Only you."
"Oh well don't I feel special!"
"I'm sorry, I had to do it. I've grown fond of you." He whispered.

I snorted, "You can't care for me, you don't even know me and trust me there's not much to love."
"I think there is," he said.
"Where's Cynthia?"
"Cynthia's gone so there's no one to help you, besides it is too late, and if anyone were to try and kill you I would get rid of them too."
I thought of the woman with gold curls, I didn't feel any remorse for her. Why?
He walked closer to me and I could see his face, suddenly taken aback by his beauty.

My blood pulsed hot and my throat burned more now, it was beginning to feel like someone was plunging a jagged knife down it.
My heart didn't move, but it would have gained speed any other day. It stayed still.
How did he cause such physical symptoms?

135

Even when I was dreaming, and he was a blood thirsty… Then I remembered what I had seen. I walked over to him and pulled his coat collar down and saw the old faint tattoo on his neck. I traced it with my fingertips.

He turned now inches from my face.

"What's your name?" I asked my mood suddenly changing. I cut him off before he answered.

"Before you were this I mean."

"I don't remember it was many years ago."

"Please I need to know."

"It started with an S I think, at least that's all I remember from him."

I froze there, hearing him and thinking it gave me that cold heavy feeling in my stomach, but it wasn't full of pain as usual.

He lifted his hand up and brushed my cheek, so quickly my feelings changed, and I didn't care what he did to me.

I no longer hated him.

I loved him.

It frustrated me.

I looked up into his bright red eyes and dropped my guard. He put his other hand on my waist again and pulled me closer to him.

I started breathing hard, when I really didn't have to breathe at all.

I flinched at his tight hold. I was speechless.

I reached up and felt his face, and then his lips; it was something I had been wanting to do for a long time. He slowly kissed me this

136

time and I felt the passion in it. Then with a strong force, I kissed him back, our lips were cold and moved in harmony.

I couldn't fight him, I didn't want too. My will and better judgment turned against me as I fell into his trap. I put my arms around his neck and he tightened his grip on me making me spasm in my spot. He smiled and I remembered I was as strong too. I smiled back stunned by the familiar smile that had kept me alive for so long and now even dead.
 I pulled hard on him and he got serious and he pushed me against the brick wall. It didn't hurt though it should have.

He put his hands around my face and he kept kissing me powerfully. I grabbed his hair and pulled him down harder to me. My other hand rested on his chest, I could feel nothing. No heartbeat, just his cold skin and the blood that flowed through it. I held my breath. I couldn't bite him. I loved him.

As if he were reading my mind he arched his neck to me and I hesitated. I looked at his face and he urged me too. I gently laid my lips on his neck and kissed him, I kissed his neck several times and then something took over me and I kissed harder, this time a warm liquid filled my mouth and I felt alive.
 I sucked slowly and he urged me more.
 He slid his hand down my thigh and under the silky lace. His cold skin was now directly on mine, and it was somehow warm.
 Though we were both dead cold, we made each other warm.

His blood was so sweet and delicious, and it made the burning go numb.

He squeezed my leg and lifted my hips towards him. I let go of his neck and tried to stop myself from panting. We slowly slid to the floor, he was on top of me now and I looked up to his face. His fangs had appeared and we both wanted blood. I grabbed his face and hastily pulled him to my lips.

I was strong too. I thought and he smiled. He could hear my thoughts.

I could hear his too, though I didn't think he was thinking much right now. I didn't want to hear him, I just wanted him.

His fangs bit my lips and mine bit his and he sucked the blood from my lips.

I arched my back and held him tighter. Our teeth retracted and we continued to kiss. He laid me on the floor and untied my robe and ran his hand across my stomach.

I didn't want him that far.

I pulled him down to me and ripped his shirt open.

Wow I was really strong.

I threw the shreds to the floor and pulled him down to me. Our bodies were one.

We continued to kiss and our bodies intertwined. I had to stop myself. I wanted more blood but I needed to stop and think.

He heard my thoughts and urged me more, squeezing my hips toward him again.

I let go and inhaled air.

"Wait, no Seth, I mean Skye."

He gazed at me with such urging eyes and I really didn't want to stop, but did he really care for me? I was thinking differently of him.

He replied in his thoughts but I was too distracted by his body on mine.

"Then marry me, be with me forever." His voice whispered in my ear.

My mood changed again.

I wasn't trying to kill the moment, but I wanted it to be real, did he care for me? Or was this just him full of thirst? Was he crazy? That's impossible to say, he really didn't know me.

"Love, you make me feel alive when I know I'm dead. I know it seems crazy but something just happened when I was about to kill you…You, you don't believe me?" He asked, his expression fading and forehead creasing.

He looked sad and it made me sad too, I didn't want to see that look. He kissed me hard again and squeezed me, making the thought disappear again.

No, I thought. It's just you will change your mind. You won't love me in this strange way forever, it might not even last longer than this day. He got up off me and again I felt the wave of sadness come. He bent and lifted me with him and led me to the window.

"For vampires its different we never fall in love twice. I can promise you it won't change."

I stared at his lips and wanted them, but I needed to focus.
Then I heard him but his lips weren't moving.
Don't you feel that, that strange power?
I moved away and you felt pain.
I listened to his thoughts.
"Now you promise me something," he asked.
"Hmm what?" I was still speechless.
"Promise me that if you ever fall out of love with me or hate me for doing this to you, you will tell me and I will leave you to be free."

At the thought of his words I felt pain where my heart used to beat. How could I feel this pain?
He was right.
I reached my hand up to his chin and felt his lips and whispered.
"Now that can't ever happen."
"I said you have to promise," he said again.
I smiled and whispered. "I promise," and did the same in my thoughts.

∞

10. Painful eyes still watch

I watched him like the eyes of a stalker. I couldn't help it. He made me smile with everything he did.

We were in English class and I had not heard a word from Benson. I was too busy trying to hold back from laughing let alone smiling like an idiot. I was never sure why as I struggled to not watch him so intently. I seemed to be fascinated by just the way he played with his fingers when he was bored, or when he grabbed random small things like a paperclip, the loose string on carpet or a woodchip broken off of a chair.

He entertained himself as he was trying to spell out his name with potato chips. Not knowing he was entertaining me as well. If it were pretzels it probably would be a lot easier, chips were hard to break how you wanted. I could tell by the concentration on his face, he refused to give up and had to spell it out the way he wanted.

I don't know how much time had passed, but when everyone started talking I knew class was over. I only noticed because Seth was now documenting his masterpiece of four letters spelled in chips with his camera-phone. He got up flashing me a smile and pointing towards his art. I gave him a thumbs up as he walked out of the room and I felt the flash of heaviness in me.

In the cafeteria I sat watching my friends just goofing around. I did too, sometimes it was good for me to act happy or a little insane. It not only helped my disguise, but helped me distract from it to. And it actually was kind of fun to act stupid then a lifeless zombie all the time. All I had to lose was my sanity, but I was ok with that. I didn't have much left.

I grabbed my water bottle and downed a few gulps. I looked down before I put it back and without thinking smashed it down instead.

Abby gasped.

"What?" I asked knowing exactly why she seemed so devastated.

"Riley how could you! That's one of God's creatures and it never harmed you!"

I had only smashed an ant the size of a sesame seed. I looked at her, she was mad. Which was kind of funny, she didn't know how to be mad. I couldn't help laughing, Kay was too, and Seth had an incredible smile on, and he was smiling at me. Probably cause he thought the same way I did, it was just a stupid bug, its better off anyway.

"Calm down Abby." I said repeating what I had just thought, "it is better off."

"You don't know that!" She retorted babbling on.

"He could have had a family maybe he was just getting some food for his home." She went on and on.

We all stared at her till she finished. Kay then got distracted with her iPod and started dancing idiotically.

Abby grunted and stormed away.

"I think she's mad." I whispered to Seth across the table.

"Good job." He replied smiling.

I laughed and started talking to Paige even though I really didn't want too, but I watched him with the corner of my eye. He reached for my water bottle that I had just used to commit a tragic murder and tore off the label. He started folding the blue label in a million ways.

The label was interesting, there was a small wolf howling under the brand name, I ignored Paige's ramble and turned to him amused. He folded it till it made a diamond shape with the wolf on the front, he took a tooth pick off the table and punctured a small hole. No one seemed to notice what he was doing. He must be so bored I thought. He then grabbed from his lap a long piece of some sort of wire string he had been playing with, in a matter of seconds made the once useless items into a work of art, a necklace that looked as if a five year old had made accidently, but I loved it.

I laughed of course.

"It's beautiful, definitely something I would pick out at the jewelry store." I teased knowing no one would ever catch me dead in a jewelry store, but something made out of pure useless stuff and the heart and mind went into it, I would take.

"Then it's yours," he said handing it to me.

"Wow amazing!" I said excitingly.

"Yea, I know I am." He said trying to sound cool.

He did.

"Thanks I'll treasure it forever!" I added sarcastically.

I ignored all the emotions I felt inside not even bothering to sort them out. Pain, Love, Anger, Control, Joy; I put the necklace over my head and smiled.

"Well time to go." Seth said relieved he could leave the stupidity at the table.

"Dance with me." Came Kay's voice. I shook my head, she was wearing a neon green top with a girls face on it. She also wore short jeans and matching heels.

"Can you reach this thing for me over there?"

"You're taller than me Kay."

"But I'm wearing heals, I don't want to break them, there so much nicer than your sneakers."

"Ugh ok, where?"

I stood and followed her to the hallway and into a classroom.

"What do you need?"

"That bucket up there."

I got on my tip-toe and reached up for the blue bucket. I was too short, I stepped up on the cabinet's handle and the last thing I saw was the bucket hit me in the face and I felt myself fall to the hard floor. Ow, I thought now that's a way to shut my mind off. I heard Kay screaming like an idiot for someone to help. She could just come over and help me herself but she was to dumb and probably just staring at me. It also sounded like she was trying not to laugh. I was fine I just didn't want to talk. I didn't open my eyes, my head felt really heavy. I didn't want to be dizzy.

I then heard a male's voice as someone started smacking me in the face.

"Wake up! Wake up girl!" He whined.

"Don't hit her!" Kay panicked.

"My mom's a doctor. I know what I'm doing."

I reached my hand up and punched the arm that was smacking and shaking me. I finally opened my eyes and sat up. I felt around my neck for the necklace. It was intact, I was relieved as I caressed it.

"What's wrong with you? I blurted out to the brown haired boy.

"I was saving you!"

"I was fine you idiot." I got back up by myself and grabbed the bucket off the floor and handed it to Kay. The boy still stared at me bewildered.

"What is wrong with you?" He repeated.

"A lot." I replied, walking quickly out the room. My face burned from where he smacked me.

My head was spinning, I need pain killers.

"Don't take it personal, she's aggressive like that all the time." Kay said whispering to the boy with a giggle.

Why did my life seem like some wacky sitcom?

"Come on Abby let's go!"

"No, No you murderer!" I heard her respond.

"Shut up and get over here! I'm hungry." I yelled back.

"Ooh yay!" She said running towards me now.

"Food, Food, Food."

At home I was with Abby and Kay and they were spending the night, I'm not sure why maybe because Kay felt a little guilty and Abby well she was always ready to have fun, she couldn't be mad at anyone longer than a few hours. They both just demanded it, and I didn't argue. Sometimes when people were around I couldn't show emotions and that kept me distracted.

146

We ate, all of us successfully and then organized stuff in my attic. We also watched T.V and planted some things in the garden on my porch. I had a smile on, because it was cold today and I loved when the weather got cold. I recalled today's date. November twentieth.

Just one week and it would be considered Christmas time. This was a time of year that I was always happy. My whole spirit changed when it came around, people even noticed. Even without him. I probably went overboard because of the joy and excitement it brought me, I craved it. Even if it is all weirdly made me think of him. The twinkling lights that reminded me of his eyes or when I felt the cold wind hit my skin or just sipped some hot cocoa by the fire. The warmth was how he made me feel all around, but there was even more than that, I loved the music and the service on Christmas Eve. I could just, Fa, La, La, La it all away.

... "A long time ago in a small town, deep in the woods lived a little girl in her little cabin. That night something very, very bad happened. She had lost her precious, Jacket! So, she goes into the cold, dark and eerie night. Desperate to find her lost jacket, she asked anyone that came her way, but no one had seen it. Until! She comes upon a third stranger, Tall-"

The candle I held blew out and gasps filled the night. My imagination triggered as I made a story up to entertain my friends. I held a candle to my face for dramatic effect. We sat on my bed where I had had dreams of all sorts. The lights in my room were all turned off like every night but this time with candles lit. Abby was giddy and waiting for what I came up with next, while Kay sat in a position of a child bundled in covers looking scared already. I laughed knowing I had blew the candle out on purpose, they were so easily intrigued.

"I guess the spirits don't want the man tall." I lit it again and continued.

"Short, no medium height, so she asks the man if he has seen her soft beloved jacket. To her surprise the man replies that he has. Excited, but nervous, as to getting it back now, she kindly asks him if she can have it back. The man says no. I want it. As she gets closer to him she finds that he is filled with a miraculous beauty.

THEN! All of a sudden, she hears a growl, it was her stomach. She had forgotten to eat because of her missing jacket. She then realizes something strange, now she is ok with him having it because of his incredible beauty, but then they hear yet again another low growl, it's a...

"Squirrel!" – Blurted Abby.

"Umm ok a squirrel, sleeping deep in the forest that had acorns but had not yet ate, but was hungry. Just then there was another growl, and they both looked with horror-stricken eyes to see in the dark a hideous! Tasmanian devil!

The man all of a sudden gets a strong feeling that he wants to protect this girl, so he decides to do just that, but she's suddenly frightened and appalled as the once beautiful man transforms into a monstrous warlock! No longer caring for this ugly beast and only wanting her jacket, the girl runs for it as it falls off his now warlock body. And now to the warlock's dismay the Tasmanian devil also wants the jacket.

The warlock jumps on the Tasmanian and they begin fighting. As blood is spilled, bones are broken and tears are shed. The girl sits clutching the jacket to her. Then she hears a loud gross sound and she looks up to see someone had been bitten. She couldn't tell who but saw as a chunk of skin was ripped from bones and now blood seeped to the ground. She screamed. Then all of a sudden they stopped. The warlock is now shocked that. -

Abby cut in again,

"His finger nail had broken!" She squealed.

I peered up to her.

"Abby shut up!"

Kay was sitting covering her ears.

"La la la I love Jesus, you can't hurt me."

I stared at the candle in my hand again.

"Ok so his finger nail had broken. The girl confused and Tasmanian wide eyed with shock. They all knew a warlock's power is destroyed by a broken nail. So suddenly the warlock and devil decide they want to be friends. This shocks the girl so she gets up and runs, now hurtles away from them. Thinking they had now decided to kill her together, but they're not. They're both actually sad that the girl was leaving them alone when they only wanted to be her friends. Then she trips, like a stupid girl does in every story, and the warlock and devil begin to run towards her to help. She terrified and thinks there running for the kill. So she grabs a spear and aims it in their direction. But the warlock trips now too and they both instantly fall into the spear like branch; they both instantly fell to death as it plunged into their stomachs and through them. The girl was scared but relieved not knowing that they had wanted to help her and be her friend. She gets up and grabs her jacket that was now splattered with blood and green goo and puts it on and walks back to her little home in her little town... The end.

I blew the candle out again and looked at them.
"You're such a freak Riley!" Kay screamed and ran out of the room and to the living room and started switching lights back on.
"That was awesome!" Abby jumped up excited.
Kay came running back quickly...
"No, I don't want to be out there alone."

*

School, a classroom, the time or day I don't remember, all I could think of was the knotting pain in me. I laid on my bed and stared at the ceiling, the whole scene replayed over almost as if it was happening all over again.

The shock when they both walked in made me feel so stupid, it showed how pathetic I was, and how I was so dumb to love someone that loved someone else.
Just pointless...
My heart seemed to fall so steep I could have lost it. This was the person in the picture, the one I had saw across the parking lot in my dream, with my Seth, and as fate ordered and the devil laughed in my face. I sat there thinking, of course their sitting right next to me. How lovely.

The whole room was dead silent, to me at least. Everyone else well they sat in their own thoughts while they listened to the teacher.

I sat numb, drowning in my own misery and trying to breathe steady. I had never been this close and trapped in this kind of situation, other than my dreams. I felt as if there were giant weights on my chest, I was getting cold and my eyes swelled a little but I wouldn't let myself get to messed up, I had to control myself or I would explode into little pieces.

Endless minutes went by, I even felt myself trembling. I didn't want this; it was taking over me like venom. Every minute I felt another weight add on my chest. The odd feeling of being at the point of my last breath creeped over slowly; my last thought, my last image. I felt the fear of being trapped in a coffin alive or trying to breathe under water, but I never seemed to die, I was just frozen. I needed to take a long gasp of air. I couldn't tell if my heart beat was fast or slow. I controlled my eyes with every thought. They wanted to burst, I looked down to my hands that were starting to shake. I put them under my thighs to try and control them. It seemed I couldn't control anything. I hated it.

I glanced over just a second, their hands were intertwined and calm. I was a volcano about to erupt. I was a disaster inside, and a horrifying mess. I thought to run to the bathroom and try to reboot my powers of control, but I knew alone in there would just give my body the release it wanted and no doubt blow into pathetic tears.

I closed my eyes and took another deep breath. I thought of the voice in my head.
STOP!
I screamed at her, I screamed over and over.
I would overcome, mind over matter.
The minutes dragged on. I finally stood afraid that I could possibly fall over. I didn't, I walked fast and found a single bathroom.

I opened the door and slid in and locked the door, I could breathe now. I reached for the switch and flicked the light on. I turned to the mirror, what I saw only disgusted me more. I felt the release in my eyes that had been fighting with me. I wiped it away fast with my sleeve.
Are you happy! Go ahead cry! Pathetic! I don't care...
There was no use for that except making me look puffy and totally destroying my mask.
I whispered to myself and God for help. I could do this, I was strong. I could beat the only thing that got to me. I knew I could. I repeated to myself as I paced the bathroom a few times, sucked my breath in and looked in the mirror again, it was convincible for me.

Please God, help me. I need you! I closed my eyes as I felt a wave of power meet me, it felt calm, calmness was now fighting with my pain, like a magnet. And I knew I could go back. I could take control. I slowly turned the light off and opened the door. I sat there for what felt like years but was only half an hour. The calmness was helping, but I just wasn't prepared for this, it had hit me too fast.

*

I couldn't sleep that night. I tossed and turned in the darkness. Sometimes I sat up or just laid there. I rubbed my fingers together and closed my eyes but I couldn't sleep. I hoped over time the pain would ease up a little or just go away or at least I would be immune to it, but I think I just got stronger to bare it.

***

Journal Entry 259

<u>"Gray"</u>
What defines the pigment of gray?
In the middle, even, fair?
The point between light and dark, Pain and love, just enough,
after, the rain, the thunder. After, when the wind blows and it's so
cold. It's beautiful, such a sight. The calmness after the storm,
the air I breathe, the only sights I can see.
There's a warmth, I can't explain, it brings me to this place, the one
place I call home.

Where you are found.
Yet it has no location, just a feeling. It could be found only where you are. No matter where,
below the sea where no soul may see or breathe.
Above the clouds where any heart can fly or dream. But you can also find it in between.
Suffocation is painful, almost unbearable. Tied to chains, finally stand up, weeks after crawling. I start to walk but I'm yanked back down to the ground, again.
Stuck between fantasy and real life; unsure of which road to follow.
Please, to just get that limited glimpse of pure exhilaration.
But it's stolen every time I receive it, like a bag over my head and it fades too quickly to gray.
In darkness I lay, gasping to get an ounce of sleep.
Praying I won't fall to steep. In light I wait, with dreams which only hold me deceived.
Today my eyes are gray, like the sky, like my heart.
Everything appears gray.
When I embrace the colorful stone, it disintegrated to ashes. I take a step on its wonder and the yellow brick road turns to cement. Charred and scarred by the match, it slowly takes over. The flame burns through the black charcoal to gray, paralyzed in a daze.

***

11. Sticks and Stones

The castle was a dark brick red color, the enormous thick gate was made of steel, opening slowly in front of Riley. The loud screeching that came from it made her want to cover her ears, but she couldn't. Riley was tied to an old carriage. It made its way up the gateway and she was yanked with it.
 Riley looked at her hands that were tied together by a thick brown rope.

  Now entering the grounds of a humongous castle she noticed how empty it was. There was a table made of wood with chairs, and ancient gargoyles lined up in different areas. The carriage came to a halt as it arrived in the middle of the grounds. She bent over catching her breath. A man stepped out with muscles that bulged from his skin. He moved towards Riley and made *grunting noises as he did.*

Riley flinched back. He stared at her for a moment and then turned and walked away.

Riley thought he walked like a rhino. She watched him make his way to another small gate. She was alone in this place but that didn't relieve her of fear or anxiety, he was no good company. Riley pulled at the rope but it seemed useless to. The rope was so tightly tied to her hands she could feel her wrists swelling. The horses neighed, one a beautiful black with blood red wings, the other a bright neon yellow with a horn like a unicorn out of its head.

The sky was lit up like a flashlight. She had to squint her eyes to see the sun, big and close but also far out to the east. If she turned to the west she could see the moon too. Riley had a rising feeling that something bad was going to happen, and of course right when she thought it, it came.

She was startled by a loud horn, like heard in an old film, some sort of animal horn.

"All hail King James." A voice shouted down behind the castle walls.

A man in gold and red armor appeared at the balcony of stone, with thick jewels around his neck and a very annoying outlook appearance.

He stepped forward as if he was a god.

"Such a high treason you are being accused of my child." He

boomed down at her through another animal part. Riley shouted back a response of confusion but couldn't be heard, no one could hear what she wanted to say. She continued to get more aggravated at not just being tied but also not being able to move or be heard. "You have committed a crime that deserves a punishment so torturous you will beg for mercy. You should be ashamed you greedy, heartless piece of dirt. You are nothing but that."

The king then spit in the air to show his disgust.
"Useless and a horrifying sight to my eyes"
Riley stood raging with confusion knowing there was nothing she could do or say, forced to endure the words that came out. A rage raised in her, she did not like to be accused of anything. King James went on in a tone of knowing exactly what he was speaking of. As if it were true, even if he were wrong, but he was right, because he was a King.
"You're better off me finding you now young one and ending what you could have started. You are not old and wise like me. You are just a stupid child that's brain has not yet started working, so you abide by my rules. Since you have disobeyed me you must suffer a greater death then your own God had planned."

Riley was breathing hard to the point if she were free she would take a knife and surely stab him right through the heart just to shut him up. Then a lot of things happened at once.
A man interrupted.
"My lord, but she has not done anything wrong, anything that anyone else would not. How could she have disobeyed?" A soft

confused voice asked behind the king.
Riley was too mad to hear him.

The king then snapped his fingers and the next thing she saw was a body thrown so suddenly over the balcony and to the floor beside her. Her eyes widened to the sight of a broken man. His eyes a dead blue, unmoving.
The whole place went erratic then. Riley grabbed the man's knife in his gold belt, her hands grasped dark oozy blood as she fidgeted to cut free from the ropes, but she couldn't get free, the knife magically disintegrated in her fingers.
Another man shouted in her defense and an army of men and woman seemed to invade the castle grounds. She looked up to see him run at the king but was abruptly stopped and collided by a distorted demon. She watched it attack the man, sinking its green sharp teeth into his neck. Blood trickled over the man's chest as he screamed in defeat.

There was no escape for Riley. The grounds of the castle were crowded with war all around. She did her best to hide from the chaos. The horses were spooked, she watched the black one with wings fly off and the neon one ran full speed away stabbing what looked to be a humungous Cyclops. With big hands holding a big wooden stake smashing it down on a woman trying to get away. The monster jerked back and roared with anger, he grabbed the horse and threw it across the battle field, and it landed on all fours as it continued to run around panicked.

She watched with no power to do anything; as usual, but explode inside. The woman crawled away with a huge gash that pulsed blood on her back. She wanted to help the woman so badly, but that thought stopped as Riley saw something strange, a shadow or movement that she couldn't place, and the woman no longer crawled away in pain, but rose with a disturbing posture and started to spasm as if possessed by something.

She clawed at her face as if trying to inflict pain on herself. The wind was getting stronger too, as a demon red with black eyes ran toward a man but was struck in the head with a blunt object. Riley looked up to see the stars in the sky were falling like meteors onto the earth.
Riley searched for the sun but it was gone as it had faded and disappeared out of existence.
The moon was still in sight and brighter than anyone could ever imagine. She stared at it and watched as it was slowly invaded by a red mist. There was an eerie fog everywhere now.

A huge creature swooped up two women and one man at the same time, and threw them like dolls into a cellar below the ground where once a table had been set. It flew in and the door shut above it, they filled the night with horrifying cries as you could almost see the smoke of their torment in the air. Riley wanted to run and help even if it meant being brutally murdered.
Why were these people trying to help me? Riley thought to herself. It was not doing anything but hurting themselves.

She saw another demon that blew fire like oxygen through his nose and mouth, it yelped and fire was blown into the air. She waited for a Calvary to come and save the day like every story, but no one came. The demons, monsters, spirits and creatures of all sort terrorized and murdered with no satisfaction. A younger boy ran with his small sword, she watched him wondering why he was so young. Then she spotted the possessed woman grab the boy by his hair and put the knife to his throat. Riley cried out pulling from the rope. The woman looked Riley right in the face and sneered with a scream in some demonic language. Riley relaxed when suddenly she let the boy go. Struck in the for-head twice with an arrow, a woman in a rose red corset dress held her bow high as she shot another two arrows into the possessed woman's chest. She then withered away.

The woman with the bow was stunning with long light brown curly hair that fell down past her waist. With light green eyes that lit up her face. Riley loved the boldness in her expression. She spoke to the boy in a language Riley didn't understand. She then turned and struck another beast with an arrow that was farther than her own eyes could reach.
She spoke a few more words to the boy and then disappeared as did the boy.

The king walked fast through the battle field, his guards attacked anyone that came near. He was making his way towards Riley. She noticed and tried to pull back again. A sword laid covered in dirt and blood from the ground, she reached and tried to get it. He charged closer and drew his sword and aimed it in her direction.

She gasped in shock, she struck him in the chest and her sword went straight through. He was even angrier now, but nothing happened. Nothing pierced skin, no blood fell from this wicked king. He then surprisingly laughed. She moved back as the sword fell to ashes on the floor. Riley knew this king could not be destroyed. She was going to die now. She got up and stood there waiting for him to kill her. He didn't, not just yet anyway.
"Oh foolish child! How dare you! Try to strike me? The king! You must know nothing of my power, so stupid and wicked." His face raged again with anger.
"Who the hell do you think you are? I am king! You will answer me! ...Open your damn mouth girl!"

He roared his words in her face. She glimpsed back without expression. Her mind had wondered to its happy place. And it was quiet. She couldn't hear what his words meant as he continued to accuse and try to break her down. She wouldn't budge. Mentally Riley had left this place.

She came to when she felt a pressure in her lower stomach. She looked down to see his hands gripping his sword now halfway gone and in her body. There was no physical pain.

The king was so angry she knew if he could he would breathe fire. A woman on the battlefield stopped at that moment of the sight of Riley. She let out a piercing cry that hurt and felt like it could explode the brains of everyone. Everyone covered their ears, the battle had frozen and all the demons and fighters stopped. They watched Riley and the King.

The clouds in the sky were moving fast and the wind was even stronger. A yellow mist fell fast from the sky and raced through like a thick cloud that was alive, it moved through the battlefield.

The demons fell to ashes and the evil spirits vanished. The people who had come to her rescue rose with confusion and excitement.

Riley and the King locked eyes with one another as she held the ashes that were once his sword.

He was alone and scared now.

Riley smiled in relief.

The mist then charged at the king and she shouted in fear, the rope came free on her bruised wrists.

∞

12. The Blaa Days

The sun was blazing down on our faces, I had to keep lifting my hand to wipe away the sweat that build up on my forehead.

Christmas was here and gone. I think it was because something was missing and I wanted it this year more than anything.

"Ugh, come on bus hurry up!"

We had left my apartment and started walking at 2. I had made sure we would get to the stop at 2:10 to make the 2:20. Or maybe even 2:30 it had to come one of those times.

"Watch the bus not come!" Abby exploded.

I stared at her while I covered my face with my big book bag.

"It will come don't worry," I assured her.

"If not 2:20 then 2:30."

"Yeah or 2:40!" she replied with doubt all over her face.

Her straight blond hair blew when a small breeze came.

"Oh nice." She said enjoying it with her long arms in the air, almost hitting some woman walking by.

"Be careful Abby! And why must you be so negative, have a little faith, if you give it time it will come, And if you must 2:45."

"No, no," she smiled.

"3."

I opened my jaw wide.

"Oh my gosh 3?!"

"But, but you said, and I was going in order," -I cut her off

"Um no Abby you said 3 not 2:50."

"That's awesome Riley."

"You're so negative I don't even want to look at you."

I moved my bag in my view of her.

She laughed some more. I liked to make Abby laugh, it made me feel useful. The bus came at 2:30 I was right again.

"Where are we going anyway?"

I glared at her again with the, are-you-serious-look.

"To our youth bible study." I replied.

"Oh yeah, ok just making sure."

We stood now on our second bus stop, waiting for a bus or taxi. It was loud and busy throughout the streets, even more then the first stop, but we hid behind a big cement pole and waited.

"Hey look at that!" Abby pointed towards a power line with birds perched on it. It was about 30 feet from where we stood on the sidewalk.

There were 4 black birds, two close together. One was a few feet away from the love birds, and one farther away on the line.

"Look, look at him."

I said frustrated and pointed towards the one creeping on the bird couple. "He's going to try and break them up."

"Oh no that just makes me just sick and angry. Someone always has to start something. Why can't they leave them alone and happy." Abby showed her anger through her voice.

"I know what a loser!" We both exaggerated.

"He should go be with that lonely bird." She continued pointing to the lonely bird on the left.

"Yeah," I agreed frowning, and then I thought and we both blurted out.

"No wait." I laughed.

"No he needs to leave her alone, happy and single, all he will do is mess up her life and then she will end up depressed and slam herself into a door."

We both laughed again, "Oh taxi!"….The taxi smelled like tobacco and sweat. It was a dark yellow pee not a clean shiny yellow like a normal taxi should be, even though a lot of them were usually very well kept in New York. This one was dirty.

The driver scanned us both down when we got in.
I stared back until he looked back onto the road.
"Where to?" He asked with a Latin accent.
"The Calvary on Oak Street please." Abby said as if she was announcing it.

She clicked a million buttons on her phone. I gazed at all the street signs and saw a man playing guitar on the sidewalk. I could tell he wasn't that good but it was nice to see. Too bad I couldn't hear him close up. I observed the inside of the taxi, there was always at least one weird looking thing hanging on the rear view mirror. I examined the monkey key chain that hanged from a chain along with one of those tree air-fresheners.

The monkey was definitely the random thing in the car besides some stickers with Spanish jokes written on them. My whole scenery vanished as I stared at the plastic brown monkey, and now I was replaying a memory in my head.

... *It was silent now and dark, no cars honked all through the streets, there weren't people all over anymore. The sun wasn't blazing down onto the car. No more trees shadowed the tips of my eyelids. Besides the silence I could hear a distant TV playing and the occasional static sound that came from an old TV with those bunny ears. The familiar dark hallway with* mirrors and those creepy wooden doors lined up the hall. I could almost smell that funny peanut butter scent. A door to the far right, half opened showed 2 small kids laughing at the television; they sat close enough to it. You would think they weren't even catching everything.

"Hey," the boy whispered.

"You think we can steal some crackers from the lunch room, or popcorn?"

"Oh and some yummy soda," the girls face lit up with mischief.

They both giggled at their thought of possibly stealing; as their eyes stayed glued to the screen, unless they glanced at one another smiling. Their eyes glowed in the dark room.

"I'll be right back ok." The small girl stated, standing up and tip toeing out of the room.

She returned minutes later with a small box of animal crackers and water in two cups.

"It's not much," she frowned passing him a cup and a full hand of crackers.

"Hey it's fine, thanks babe." He said proud of his friend.

"Hey don't call me that!"

"What?" He asked surprised.

"Babe," she replied; her cheeks red like cherries but her face firm.

"Why not?" He asked going on as any persistent guy would.

"Because you're not allowed, you're just a boy, and only my boyfriend can call me that." She said with a serious tone, biting off the head of an animal cracker.

"You don't have one!" He said rolling his eyes.

"Yeah but I will one day and then he can call me that." She gazed at him with a childish grin.

He gazed at her for a long minute smiling with his big white shining teeth.

"Ok," he replied. Sticking half of his crackers in his mouth. They both turned their focus back on the TV just inches away.

They watched the boy run away from the bad guys in the movie with his friend the monkey. The fat bad guy tripped on a banana and they both jumped up laughing....

"Riley hello we are here let's go!" A voice was saying in the background. Snapping out of it now all the noise from the streets came back and the kids laughing drifted away like a breeze.

"How are you all doing today?" Paul asked, looking us each down.

"Fine," we chorused.

He stopped at me and asked again.

"I'm fine." I replied faking a smile.

I wasn't fine, I thought to myself. I had not seen Seth in three weeks.

I wanted to see him for a few minutes, even if we didn't talk or just exchanged a few sentences. I needed to see his smile, his bright fathomless eyes, and a quick hug or to hear him say my name. It has been too long, and the last time I saw him was beginning to fade, and I needed another picture of him to store in my head…

What was really cool about our youth leader was that he didn't come with a lesson for us like all the teachers; he just came with his Bible and his wisdom. Paul would just start talking and giving advice, or he would let anyone ask a question or help on a problem, and he always had an answer.

Another thing I loved that other teachers didn't have was that he really cared. He didn't treat us like a bunch of young teenagers. He treated us all equally like himself. Paul knew that everyone had issues and he seemed to know how to help us without even knowing he was. Every time we had a bible study I listened very carefully and some things he said clicked for me and stayed in my head. I described Paul as a man with a mind of a 400 year old, a body of a 40 year old and a heart of a 4 year old.

Today 3 quotes hit me hard.

1. *"You see we strive for something but sometimes it's not God's plan for you, we collect and save it because you want it so bad but all it does is just rot and becomes like a foul smell in you."*

2. *"You can't leave what's in your head behind, you can't make a break from it, no matter where you go or what you're doing it's going with you like luggage. It might be a*

new scenery around or different people but you can't ever change or get rid of what's in your heart. To do that you need him."

3. *"When we lie it is because we are afraid we won't be loved anymore."*

I thought of the calmness that came over me that time in the bathroom, it had felt like a big shot in my heart. The injection had taken its course and the drugs numbed you everywhere, a strange calmness.

*

"Hey that's my crayon!" Whined Juli at her little brother Milly. I watched her snatch the crayons away and hold them close to herself.

"Guys, be nice come on, color with me." I was babysitting for a woman in my church.

"Ok you guys it's the time your mom said you have to go to bed."

Milly jumped and screamed at the top of his lungs.

"Oh jeez shhh."

"Um Riley, can I call you Rie Rie."

"Sure Juli." I couldn't help but smile at these kids. Her eyes lit up.

"Yay I like you Rie Rie."

"I like you too."

"Hey Rie Rie, can we go to bed 2 minutes after we're supposed too?"

"It already is," I laughed.

"Well how about 3 more, please, please, please."

"Ok, ok, just stop bouncing in your chair like that you are going to fall."

"Yay!" She squealed.

Juli is six years old and Milly two, they were funny with personalities already rising in them.

Juli was still smiling at me.

"What?" I asked.

She laughed.

"I don't know I just like smiling at you."

I smiled back.

"Alright guys time for bed." I glanced at Milly, good no scream. Juli rushed with her crayon on the page and closed the book.

She stood up, "Come on Milly." We ran to their small bedroom with toys thrown all over the floor.

"Into bed," I ordered them both.

"Throw me in!" Juli squealed again.

"Ok," I laughed.

These kids were just too good.

Milly was crawling into his small dinosaur bed.

"Ok goodnight you two, sweet dreams."

I flicked the light switch off, closed the door but left it a crack open, like they had asked. I went back to the living room, and opened a book I had got at the library.

"Rie Rie." I heard a small voice say. I jumped and skipped to the room.

"Yes what is it?" I whispered.

"Um...I can't sleep."

"Well, what do you usually do to fall sleep?"

"Well," Juli replied in a squeaky teacher like voice.

I stood by her bed. Milly was lying on his bed with toy cars in his hands as he came close to falling asleep.

"I usually just lie down and fall asleep right away."

"Well just do that then Juli."

"I can't," she said poking me in the ribs with her foot.

"Why?"

"Because there is a babysitter here."

"Come on your mom will be home soon, I don't want anybody getting in trouble."

Juli grabbed onto two of my fingers and laid down. I glanced at Milly and he gave me a big smile, with his brown hair and light skin.

"Shh." I mouthed putting my index finger to my lips. Turning back to Juli, she had her eyes closed and seemed to already be peacefully sleeping.

She was so adorable, long curly brown hair and big brown eyes hiding under her eye lids. They slowly opened and gawked at me.

"Rie Rie, can I ask you something? I almost forgot and I have to ask you now."

"What is it?"

"Do you know how to spell?"

"Yes."

"Ok good can you please give me an h-u-g?"

"Aw, come here." She reached for me with her small arms and hugged me tight. I felt like not letting go of her. She reminded me of myself when I was little.

"Ok, ok time to sleep now. You got school tomorrow. Close your eyes ok."

"Ok Rie Rie, but I really don't like school."

"Hmm...me and you both kiddo."

The whole house was silent this time. I sat on a big green couch in the small living room so I could flip through the channels. I settled on an old *Sci-Fi* movie. I laid back and tried to relax and empty my mind. I could probably re sight the words to this movie. I had seen it almost a hundred times.

I watched the adorable boy confessing his un-denying love for his girl.

Why didn't they just be together? They both loved each other but weren't together.

With a passion it sickened me.

"I cannot live a lie".... her exact words.

She would have him!!!

Wow was I seriously yelling at her in my head. Before I could continue to argue over her decisions my phone rang and I answered it still arguing over the movie in my head. "Hello, yes? What happened?"

*

The heart monitor filled the whole room. I stood in the small white closed in walls of the hospital; nervous, afraid, and relieved.
There was a TV mounted high that played some old movie that I have never seen. A woman laid beaten in a dark room. I could hear her whining for help; besides the loud sounds coming from the heart monitor.
I hated hospitals, everything about them. Many people have died here. I didn't like the idea of hundreds of people sick in one building.
I took care of myself when I got sick. Never enough to where someone would make me go, and if they tried it would be kicking and screaming. Besides the death, there was the piercing bright lights that burned my eyes and the white linoleum hard floors. What were they trying to make it look like, a psych ward? Then there was the worst part, the smell.
A mixture of latex gloves, rotted apples and vomit. It was freezing cold, apparently it helps kill germs.
Hospitals appeared clean but the smell was nauseating, and

in some areas there was the strong nose burning scent of bleach or chlorine. I focused on what was in this room to distract myself from the foul scent. There were two chairs and a table with magazines sprawled on top.

Then the small hospital bed that seemed as if it could barely keep anyone warm or comfortable. On that hard bed laid a person I hadn't seen in years. It was Luna, with her dark coco skin and brown short hair that stopped at her shoulders. When college started we seemed to drift slowly away. I guess because I decided on a different one then her; the one where Seth was. I didn't like that; I was always strict with the saying, best friends forever. I'm supposed to be the loyal friend, it was my fault, I was too wrapped up in my pathetic problems; that I didn't pay attention to what was happening.

Most of the time I couldn't really stand people I just wanted to be alone; everyone except Seth, but I realized that there were a few friends that need me and I needed them too.
I was going to fix this lost connection with Luna. The second I heard she was in the hospital from a car accident and had surgery from an internal problem that had occurred. I panicked like I did for everything.

I knew I was probably being selfish but I needed her right now. More than anything I knew that I could trust her. More than any friend I knew. I could be totally honest for once. I had been feeling like a bomb that could explode at any given second. I knew I was supposed to do this.

I stared her down not sure if I should just wait for her to wake up or shake her and yell her name in excitement, but I didn't have to do either. Her brown eyes flickered slowly. Luna's face lit up and she squealed my name.
"Oh Luna I missed you!"

She jumped up so excited.
"Hey be careful you just had surgery a few days ago."
"I'm just fine how have you been Riley?"
"Me, how are you, you're the one in the hospital."
"I swear I am fine just a little pain, no big deal."
She looked ok besides the grogginess.
"No offense Luna, but you look high." I observed her tired eyes and weird laugh.
"Ow, ow I cannot laugh." She said holding her side.
"So tell me everything." I said avoiding her question. I listened to her tell me what has been going on since we last saw each other.
"So how is Seth? And Kay, Abby, the whole gang?"

I immediately tensed up hoping she wouldn't notice.
"Um, fine." I replied fighting and debating with myself. I knew Luna, if she caught on she would beat it out of me regardless of the pain or needle in her arm. I changed the subject and laughed.
"Luna you're wearing two hospital gowns, that's funny."

"I know," she laughed and got serious again.

"So do you still see Seth a lot?" She grilled me down for a story. "Yeah we go to the same college and hang out once in a while. Well actually he hasn't been around lately."

I flashed my eyes away from the bright white lights covering my nose from the smell that got stronger when I moved.

"Come on tell me what's been going on, I know there is something."

"Well," I smiled. "I'm reading this book." I reached down in my bag for it. "It's so good I love it, I should tell you there's this—"

"Riley!" She cut me off.

"Oh sorry, well I have been working a lot lately too."

"Mhmm." She replied. "Come on your turn, you know you can trust me."

Dang it I thought, crap, crap, crap, she's got me. I couldn't decide what I wanted to do.

"You don't want to know Luna. My life is just the same as anyone, but I am ok."

"Riley." I looked at her with a long stare and thought. Maybe she wouldn't remember the next day. Especially with how drugged she was. I tried to change the subject again.

"Hey do they have you on something?"

"Yeah this breathing thing, not sure what's in it though."

"Nice," I replied staring at the floor and fidgeting with my fingers. "Riley—"

"Luna you know that popular song on the radio about that girl who loves her friend but she don't tell him..."

"Yeah I think, but I don't see how....oh. I think I know what's going on."

I felt an anxiety shock creeping on.

"I got to know that I can trust you Luna, with my life. You can't say a word. You would never know how important this is to me." She put her hand to her mouth like we did when we were younger.

"Locked away forever," she said turning her fingers as if she was turning a key. I felt so stupid like a kid with a little secret, but it was so much more than that. I didn't even know how to explain it to myself.

"I think I know who this is about."

"No, no you don't."

"No, but I think I do."

I smiled and smiling kept me from showing the torture.

"What you're not going to tell me, come on Rie."

"I need you to hide that key far behind the lock. It needs to be in a lock that can't ever be opened."

"Of course Riley...is it Seth?"

"Shh pshh ...no, no way! ... Seth the humorous, hot shot, big headed, conceited, no way Luna."

I was lying horribly for the first time.

"Riley, I know what it feels like to have a guy, you love so much, you feel that no one could ever possibly understand, to know that you would do anything for him, and he just seems to never get it; please you cannot leave and not tell me. I know you want to! Come on; I see it eating at you."

I laughed, hiding what I wanted to say as I felt my eyes get heavy.

"What's the matter you need some gossip, cooped up in this place too long?"

"Yes!"

She threw her hands into the air.

"Ok, ok, ok, ok, ok you're right." I whispered covering my face and staring at my black and white converse.

"Seth." I whispered.

I didn't even want to look at her, I felt...ashamed, which surprised me.

Why was I ashamed?

"Why don't you tell him?" She asked.

"You know you will one day, when you can't keep it in any longer."

I glanced up now full of words. As I blabbed to her things I could never tell anyone. I didn't feel relieved but I felt a slight lift off my mind and chest and the loud voices were now becoming whispers again. We talked for another hour and I was finally able to stand up, positive that she fully understood everything.

"We're going to hang out more right? I need you to talk to Luna, you just put yourself in this so be prepared for me to desperately need you."

"Of course I am always here, well not here, I hope I get out soon but you know how to reach me."

"Yup, thank you Luna I needed this, get well and remember the key stays behind the lock."

"Yup," she replied.

"Wow I love Seth." I said it out loud for the first time. It feels weird saying it out loud, not even by myself would I say it.

"See don't you feel better, relieved and happy like all the weight has been lifted?"

"No." I replied. "I feel...terrified."

∞

13. How ironic

"She's burning up we have to cool her down." I couldn't move or barely breathe. All that went through my mind was that this is it; my time to go.

I could hear people shuffling around everywhere. My eyes were slammed shut. They hurt too much to open, when I tried there was just a piercing white light that made me think that I had reached heaven; but I didn't want to go yet, I didn't want to go just yet, anyway. I was being slammed down on a hard cold surface. People shouted from all directions but none were familiar. I wanted there to be at least someone I could recognize, but all the voices were strangers.

Cold fingers touched my wrist and neck. I had an urge to push them away, but I felt too weak and heavy to move at all.

Someone tore at my clothes which frustrated me. Heavy sheets like brick blocks hit my skin, it felt like a belly flop in a pool. My face, chest, stomach, arm and legs were covered in ice packs. I felt all the skin on me pricked up; wincing at cold needles in my arm. Three more stabbed through, in my finger, in my arm, and then again. I didn't know if they were connecting or putting stuff in me or taking my blood but it hurt.

"It's going down now." He may have announced in my head. Go away I thought. I once again heard the irritating beeping from the monitor.

"Heart rate is steadying." I heard someone say.

"Doctor," a woman whispered. Fingers checked my pulse again as the cold feeling came off. They lifted the packs off leaving me bare again. Then breathing seemed to get harder.

"What's wrong with her," a nurse asked.

"I...don't know exactly. It's just happening, I can't find the cause, the blood results?"

"Negative on everything."

I felt pains in my chest and I started to spasm where I laid.

I was choking, it felt like someone had stuffed a sock in my mouth.

"Hypoxia doctor!"

"Get the bag," the hands touched my pulse again. I gasped out a name the only one I wanted to hear; but also the least most too, but something in me did want him here. I choked out the name again before anything covered my face. Another voice came from far away.

"No family," but I will check her phone for the name."
 No, I tried to get out but couldn't. He can't know, he can't come here and see this.
"It could be a Pulmonary Embolism?" the nurse suggested. "If that's the case she could go into cardiac arrest."
"We will get it ready just in case." Another said. How many people were here? I thought.

Someone held something over my face, I felt the air being forced into my lungs, and then I felt something strange. My heart pace changed, I was used to the sudden freeze of it, the heaviness or the occasional abnormal speed; but right now it was slowing; until it was a faint echo. The voices all rose.

"She's crashing!" Someone kept repeating the monitor numbers. Everything seemed really gone but not at the same time. I felt as if I wasn't in my body anymore. As if I was floating in the air but at the same time I was still in my body. Then a three-hundred pound man I guessed; drove the heels of his hands into the center of my chest, while others still poked needles into me.

Like I was some kind of experiment. I had a feeling that someone in the room was preparing to send four-hundred watts of electricity throughout my body, a door opened at that moment and then a woman spoke.
"You can't be in here boy."
"What the hell. You called me here lady. What is wrong with her?"
I jolted up, breathing in oxygen again. More pain came as I seemed to completely return to my body.

No! I screamed in my head.

I tried to reach my arm out; it was too heavy. "She wants to tell me something." The voice spoke making me calm.

> *My pulse, heart, and breathing all slowed to a normal pace*
"No, boy," the nurse said again.
"You need to wait outside, she is stable now."
"She is ok then?" He asked seeming frightened and starting to leave. No, no the voice in my head begged.
Oh shut up and wake up already Riley

*   *"Doctor, doctor." the boy was gone. They moved in to start the process again."*

* *"Wait!" the young nurse in the room shouted. "Bring him back in here."*
"What why?" The doctor asked loudly.
* *"I have a crazy hunch." She replied and the door opened again.*
"Hey boy come back here." Someone yelled down the hallway.
"She's going to die!" The doctor roared.

* Wait." The young nurse said again. The voice came again and came closer.*

*   *"Look doctor, look at her now... she is stable."*
"What the?" The doctor was amazed.
"The boy stood awkwardly by her." I think you need to stay with her right now." The nurse said, it sounded like she was grinning.
"Haha I know I have that effect on people," the voice spoke. She knew he had a smirk. They checked all her vitals again but for some strange reason. Nothing was causing these symptoms. She didn't go into cardiac arrest again. She was stable, no fever.

"That boy is the reason why she is still alive." He stood unsure if he should touch her; maybe that would help.

"Nah. Just a coincidence." He said to himself.

I laid peaceful and calm, I felt fine now but wanted to be invisible. He needed to leave. He shouldn't be here.

"I kind of have to go." He said out loud again to anyone in the room.

"I can't just stay here. It's not doing anything."

"I think it is," the nurse spoke.

He rolled his eyes

"Ok fine." He said taking a seat.

He was only here because he felt obligated, not because he wanted too.

Stupid heart I thought. Just go away. Why was he like this in this dream? I asked myself. Three seconds later I regretted even thinking it…why couldn't he magically just want to be with me…why?

I shouldn't even be thinking that. I knew there were questions the world had and they would never find reason or truth. Some questions just won't find their answers.

*

I heard myself calling his name softly, I knew already that I was lost in a dream. I found myself screaming his name; it shocked me, so much that I cut myself off and covered my mouth with both hands.

What was I doing? Spinning, everything moved in all directions. I felt I was going to fall over. I tried to grab onto something to stand still, but I couldn't. Everything moved too fast. There was a human shadow in my view.

A dark figure slowly walked away from me, I tried to walk after him but tripped and fell on the wet concrete. The drizzle of rain fell onto my skin washing the blood on my scraped hand away. I struggled to get back up. The brick walls of the tunnel were closing in. He had stopped and turned back toward me. I felt nauseous and my head pounded from the dizziness.
"Come back." I whispered.

He stared down at me as I stumbled to reach him. He looked at me and I held the ground with my bloody palm, steadying myself so I could read his expression. It was wrong. I held onto my position and scanned his face. For the first time I couldn't understand why he looked at me, why he stared down at me with such... disappointment.

I never thought I would see that in his face.
What had I done? I avoided ever seeing that. It made me sick.
"No, no." I whispered.
"Please stop!"
He peered down on me with disproval. He shook his head and began to walk off again.
"No please! I tried, I tried!" – My scenery vanished, and there was a bright sun light that now beamed on me...

"I can't believe you lied to me all this time." The sun burned down in the parking lot.

"I thought we were friends Riley!" Here he was angry.
"We are that's why I couldn't! –
"No, it's all a lie, and I trusted you!" His voice was so loud.
"Please don't hate me, I need you."
"Now I know, you really are crazy! We're not friends anymore, I don't even know what you are to me." His words repeated and mixed up in my mind over again, they turned threatening as if like a scary children's rhyme.

"I'm sorry..." I didn't know what else to say, I never prepared myself for this situation. I didn't want to think this would happen. I thought I could prevent this. He shook his head cursing under his breath. Hundreds of birds flew over us, everything vibrated and gained strength. The grass and trees rustled so fast I could hear them. The winds speed grew and grew. The clouds raced in the sky like cars. With anger and disgust he turned walking away again.
"No!!!!" I screamed at the top of my lungs, over and over. But he couldn't hear me, or didn't want to. Maybe he tuned me out or the wind was just too loud. The wind whistled as it blew by through the trees, leaves fluttered all around. Car doors slammed shut, not just his, but every car in the lot. The alarms and horn went off blaring in the air. I screamed until nothing came out. And then once again my scene changed...

I sat curled up in a corner with my hands on my ears. He laughed.

His laugh vibrated through my whole body, I quivered where I sat. I couldn't hide, though I tried. Sticking my face in my knees and pressing my hands hard over my ears to drown it out. But it didn't work.

Whispers grew louder as the laughing continued.

"I knew it!! You're so pathetic… and stupid. Hahahaha." I looked up but all I saw were evil smiles from all directions. The bathroom smelled and was dirty. The toilets flushed repeatedly and the sinks flowed water. The paper towel dispenser seemed to come alive as the paper towels flew out into the air falling flat on the ground. I was surrounded by dozens of Seth's that laughed and taunted me. They wouldn't stop laughing.

"Stop, stop, stop!!!" Please stop!!!" Everything finally went silent…

Silent and dark. I sat up in my bed.

"Stop, stop, please don't go! Please don't- I whispered. But nothing filled the quite room. The slight moon light showed in through the window. The rain fell softly and tapped the window. It reflected a shadow on the walls of my room. Dotted shadows, they appeared like bugs.

"What's wrong love?" A voice as soft as a winter breeze, whispered in the dark. A smooth but firm hand touched my elbow gently. The majestic fingertips lingered as I spun around in his direction.

I felt the air knock out of me at his sight. I had a quick flash of sudden jealousy. How did he do that to me? And not even knowing.

"Umm nothing just another bad dream, I'm okay."

"You always say that," he replied sitting up in the big bed beside me; I felt his body heat under the covers and it made my stomach lurch. He gave me his sly smile in the dark. "What happened?" He asked again.

"I'm okay really its stupid."

"Hey nothing you say is ever stupid, it's as important as my love for you, and that is very. Magnificent." I laughed.

"That would sound so corny if someone else said it."

"Heyyy," he playfully whined.

"That's good." I smiled.

"And I'm fine really."

He got serious again.

"Tell me now," his expression drove me crazy. I sighed aloud on purpose.

"Okay, you didn't want me… You were – and hated me and then laughed." I felt my stupid eyes get puffy again.

"Oh love," he reached up his hand to my face and held it. "Not those nightmares again. Look at me Riley."

I was, I thought.

I couldn't stop staring up into his eyes.

"Now breathe," he reminded me. I smiled and let out my breath. "I'm never leaving you, you're my wife and a part of me, never. I'll keep telling you this every night if I have to, I just wish you didn't doubt it. I hate seeing you like this."

I didn't even notice I was staring at his chest, I had to if I wanted to pay attention to his words.

"I'm sorry." I whispered.

"Don't, it is okay." His voice was so reassuring. Both hands held my face firmly but so gently, he pushed my hair back. "Now look at me and smile, you know you want to. You will, I know you can't look at me without smiling. All you got to do is look at me, really look at me love. Let me see those eyes." He begged. I looked up again, and of course my smile was as wide as possible. He leaned in and kissed my for-head. Closing my eyes as I tried to calm my heart rate. I felt his lips on my eyelids and then a quick one on my mouth.

"Riley?"

"Hmm, what, I'm here, yes?" I replied dazed and lost, forgotten of the nightmares that had come. He gestured laying back down on the bed.

"You can lie down with me the way you like to, even though I prefer holding you." I quickly got next to him before he changed his mind.

I laid my head on his chest to feel his beautiful heartbeat in my palm and ears.

"I love to hear your heartbeat when I sleep."
He chuckled. "I know, you tell me all the time."
He held me to him and began to softly sing in my ears. It was the sweetest song I had ever heard. He stroked my hair

as he sung me to sleep. Making sure no hair fell in my face. I didn't think I could ever sleep, not like this. Was he really going to sing to me? He would have to all night. I didn't want to sleep, not now. His singing lowered to a low humming.

"Close your eyes and have sweet dreams my love." He whispered. I obeyed and very slowly started to drift off, his humming got louder, suddenly his hands were now around my neck, he continued to hum. His hands squee*zed and tightened around my neck. It started getting harder to breathe. My hands tried to pull his away from my throat. I started to gag. I felt pressure in my face as he choked me, still humming. I did not understand what was happening. I tried to speak, nothing came out. I struggled more. Seconds went by. My vision became dark, his humming the only thing I could hear in my ear. I let go of his hands, I stopped fighting. It all went black. I was dead.*

*

My eyes flashed open to the sudden bark of a dog; the room was lit up with sunlight as Jack barked out the window. I lifted my head up and then slammed it into my pillow. I cursed. I had deceived myself, something, I rarely do. I was smarter than that. I felt the stupid uncontrollable pain come over me as I cursed in my pillow...

∞

14. To many confrontations

"Hey Riley."

Shoot, how did she sneak her way towards me? Did I look friendly? I sat in the far back of the cafeteria. My hair in my face and earphones blasting in my ears, the total don't talk to me look. Apparently it didn't work. And this just wasn't one of my friends, this was Ivy.

"How are you?" She sat down in front of me, her purple feathery skirt moving in circles. I kind of liked her long sleeve black denim jacket. I didn't say it though.

"I'm fine." I replied. "Just going to go home soon, watch a movie I guess."

"Oh that's cool," she said in a weird tone. I didn't like it and I had a feeling whatever she was going to tell me would upset me somehow. I couldn't help it if it did.

"What's wrong?" I asked with my full attention on her.

Her face saddened with negativity.

"It's just, well stupid, one of my ex's is getting to me, I miss him but I am sure you're used to hearing this."

My stomach tightened. "Sorry Ivy that really sucks, do you want to talk about it?" The look she gave me made me instantly know who she was referring to.

"Well you know who he is, he's well your best friend."

"Oh," I replied at a loss for words. Her tone seemed to bother me but she didn't notice at all; I mean if that was the case why would she come up to me? Then I watched the hidden frown and anger in her face. I knew if that was me, I would just look like death. This was only the second time that I have been approached with this story, but I knew what to do. I wanted to help her for some weird reason. "I'm fine really," she added. I did not understand why they came to talk to me. I was his friend. They were just EX's...

"It's cool; you want someone to talk too."

"Yeah, it's just I feel that I can't trust anyone, and well you barely talk to anyone."

"You want to hang out sometime?" I cut her off; what was I doing I asked myself. I must be insane....

*

"We should probably get back in there; we are going to

193

miss the movie and never know what happened." I said walking out of the restroom.

"Or we could just ask the rest of the guys what happened." Seth replied looking at me with his light smile.

"True, but don't you want to see for yourself? You just paid ten dollars for it." I walked over to him as I spoke.

"Hmm, no not really." I stood awkwardly by him staring down at the floor like a dummy. I traced with my eyes the green and purple swirls that were scattered on the movie theater carpet floors and walls. Every couple of feet there was a movie poster. That read either now playing or coming soon. He sat on a metal bench besides the water fountain and restroom door. All the movies had been playing for a while now so no one was really around; besides the occasional person who ran out to the restroom.

 "Riley what's up?" He sat not looking at me; he was texting on his phone.

 "Nothing really." I had no idea what to do or say.

Why did I even walk out of the restroom or even the theater; it was as if my body absentmindedly just got up and came out here when Seth did, though he didn't feel like an idiot, I bet myself. He just wanted to buy some snacks for himself. The split second I walked down the black stair way passing all the yellow lights at my feet. I came to the door that let out all the bright light and fresh popcorn smell. Unless it was the bucket he sat scarfing down like a pig; of course to me it was cute and funny. I thought about how badly I wanted to speak fluently and have basic human conversation, but I couldn't. The words I wanted vanished all too quickly like a breeze. After so many years you would think I was at least comfortable and at least able to say anything. It was so easy when we were kids. Now I was an old rusty robot. I couldn't seemed to stop asking myself the same questions every day; how I feel so small and stupid on the outside and a painful numbness on the inside; just when I was with him. When he talked to me it was as if he had some kind of cruel magic in him; making every word sound like he was an Egyptian god. I felt nothing I said could ever measure up to it. Regardless of how deep and poetic people assumed of me, it was funny how every time he told me something that I've heard before; dumb, sarcastic, or meaningful. When it fell from his lips it was as if I was hearing it for the first time.

"Well you just going to stand there like a mute, come here." He gestured waving his phone at me.
"Come sit next to me." Oh shoot I thought. I am going to die right here! Then the movie makers can make a pathetic tragic story of the girl who died in the movie theatre. I pictured what the movie poster for that would look like.

"Ok," I replied knowing I was giving him a, *don't-know-shouldn't-we-go-back-look*. Then again I was the idiot that asked for this.
"Is there something you wanted to tell me?"

"NO." I said without thinking.

"You sure?"

"Yep, tell me how you have been Seth. I have not seen you in a while." I remembered what Paul had said before.

"When we lie it's because we are afraid we will not be loved anymore."

"No-," he interrupted my thoughts. "We are talking about you!"

"I am boring, you don't want to know anything about me, but you should already know that." I said smiling in his direction.

"No you're not."

"Yes I am." I said stretching out the words to take up time. I am so boring him, I thought. It was better when he messaged me. Even though face to face was what I preferred. I was worse, so it was best to talk from a distance. I could think so much better and could use big meaningful words. Not sounding like a complete idiot. I stared at him for a long second. He texted some more. I just stared at him. *Look away, look away!* I heard that voice in my head say. I glanced away. Dang why is he so... unfathomable?

Shut up. I replied to the voice.

It went silent.

I had a twisted feeling in my stomach. I tried again.

"So how are you?"

"Just I think everyone hates me." He said out of nowhere.

"What!" I yelled out thinking that I had won by getting him

196

to talk.

"Where did that come from, are you insane? What's in that popcorn?" He smiled.

"I always mess up everything."

"That's not true Seth; I don't like you when you do that." A nod was all I got in return.

"Seth what's wrong."

"I just got this bad feeling that something is going to go wrong, it always does. I always do something or say something that drives everyone away. I don't think I am meant to ever be happy."

I felt a sharp feeling in me like a rubber band springing back at me.

"Nonsense, everyone deserves to be happy. Well except criminals, murders, rapist, and child molesters. They should never be happy, just rot in a-... Sorry I am talking too much again, you know I do that a lot you know, when I start talking."

He gazed down at me amused and I closed my mouth shut, he then laughed.

"I can say the same thing about you."

"I am happy." After a few seconds to think of a good comeback; he gave me a look and he knew I was lying.

"You'll always have me, I am making sure of that, no matter what you do or say, I am here; and everyone makes mistakes but if whoever you drove or drive away, well their stupid to let you. Not you." I said trying to reassure him.

Shh you are talking too much you are nothing more, the voice in my head said.

I know. I replied.

It was so easy being his friend. The hardest part was not being more than that.

"Hmm, thanks," he said standing up. "But I still don't believe it; come on time for the movie."

Of course, idiot he isn't going to believe you, say something really profound.

Nothing came.

I need a dictionary I thought. I asked myself another question, knowing I wasn't going to get a response.

Why was I in love with a man, maybe even more dramatically reserved then myself?

*

"What? I can't hear you!"

"I said, what do you want to eat?"

"What?"

"I'm hungry Michael!!"

"What?" Vince yelled again.

"He said he wants food!!" Kay screamed through the crowd. Everyone in the area went silent; it was like those movie moments where you hear crickets in the background.

There weren't any but we all did burst out laughing.

"Oh," Michael smiled. "Oh so am I, let's get some hot dogs."

All the guy's eyes lit up at the sound of hot dogs.

"Boys." I whispered under my breath.

Luna and Kay giggled. We started walking to the food area where it wasn't as loud.

"No dude! Let's get those big turkey legs and see how many we can eat," Michael suggested pointing to the stand.

"I want in!" Seth joined, "I will beat you both."

"Ha, yeah, right!" Vince punched him in the arm.

My eyes locked on them.

"Oh, he did not" –oh... calm down he's just joking around, Seth's laughing too. I shook my head to stop the arguing.

"Dramatic much?" I asked the voice... no response.

All three boys stood by the turkey stand as they joked about how many they would eat.

"Come on, Riley let's go on the cliffhanger ride!"

I shook my head no.

"Oh, pleeeease!" Kay begged me with her big smile.

"Luna, can you go with Kay?"

"Sure." She sang skipping to her side.

"Come on Kay, where is Abby anyway?"

"Work," Kay and I replied at the same time.

"I love it when you both reply at the same time." She laughed.

"Just be careful Luna," I ordered.

"I'm fine now Riley!" I watched them make their way to the line. I laughed out loud to myself, what was I doing at a fair? The place was way too loud for me and I mean I love loud music and concerts but this just had too much noise. Either people were screaming and laughing or there was all the racket from the games. People ran around everywhere too. I was afraid of a clown jumping up from behind me.

"Hey Rie," a voice breathed in my ear, that voice scared me

almost just as much. I felt a magnetic force in my gut.

"Hey," I replied under my breath.

"Why don't you go on a ride?"

I tried to gather my thoughts but no words came out.

"I don't like that really, the idea of spinning around in the air knowing that the only thing that was holding me up was metal and electricity. Then there is also my head spinning and the feeling of my heart being up my throat." He smiled and then I did as well.

"So what do you do here?" He asked.

"I like the games where you throw balls, drive cars or arcade kind of stuff, but I don't really like it here at all, it is too loud."

"So you play the games where you win stuff?" He asked me with a goofy face.

"I guess," I replied smiling but only because he still was.

"So who won?" I asked changing the subject and pointed at his greasy hands.

"I did of course," he smirked. "Duh I am a freaking beast. They chickened out halfway through the first leg, but you should have guessed that I would win, I mean you are supposed to be on my side, right?" Seth said awaiting my answer.

"I am always on your side Seth," I said acknowledging the fake/serious smile I got in return.

"Good you better be."

My smile disappeared and a frown shot clean across my face.

"Let me see your hand" I said suddenly.

"Why?" He smirked, putting his hand behind his back.

"Let me see your hand now!" He nodded his head no once

more.

"Why are there scabs on your knuckles?" I asked angry now. Seth rolled his eyes and tried not to look at me.

"I got mad ok." He shrugged with another smile.

"Why do you men always have to punch things to let your anger out? You just love upsetting me don't you?" I yelled.

"It's nothing, I just got in a little fight and punched some concrete."

"Why, when, are you ok?" A sudden ache of hatred for this stranger passed through me. While a slow smile spread once again across his face.

"Hey, not funny, don't do that. Please promise me you won't do this again." I asked tapping his hand lightly.

"Sorry, I can't promise that." He said still smiling, no fair I thought.

"Seth I thought you were different? I thought you were smart enough not to do that," I continued.

"I can say the same thing about you,-" He cut me off and I started breathing in deeply, what did he mean by that?

"I am just an ordinary guy Riley." He said.

"No." I firmly corrected him. "No, you're not, to me anyway."

I saw someone coming. "Hey dude, come on!" Vince gestured to Seth to leave with him. He gave me one of his hugs and I smiled, but it was only there because of the tension of the quick hold. He released me and ran off wiping his hands on his jeans. Once he left my mind began to wonder again. It was unbelievable how seeing him seemed to take me away from the misery and into a grand place, I imagined only heaven could be like. If I could I would just grab him and whisper to him the very secrets I planned to take to my grave. It was completely pointless, no matter what I cried out to him, it wouldn't be enough, it wouldn't say enough, and he wouldn't believe a word. Even if I ever did break through the prison what words could I ever put together to form something sensational. Without sounding like or feeling like an utter fool. I tripped on the hay below me; I held my ground from falling over completely.

Woah, Riley breathe. I reminded myself. I closed my eyes and took a deep breath.

What was wrong with me? Had I really just forgotten to breathe again? He is gone, breathe.

I could feel a knot tightening in my stomach pulling everything in the wrong direction. This is so stupid. I decided instead of waiting around, I would walk and explore the fair on my own. I saw the Ferris wheel a few feet away. I passed some more rides and made it to the games; like the one where you try to drop the man into a pool of water. I thought that one was amusing. I saw a couple jump in victory at winning the ping pong fish bowl game. I stopped when I heard a man's voice holler out for me to try out the basketball game, but ignored it. After I passed a few more games and the cotton candy stand, again another man stopped me. "Hey short stuff." This time I paid attention. I came to a halt and turned in his direction. He held the rings that people stood tossing trying to get around the beer bottles. I gave him an annoyed smile.

"Want to try?" The stranger asked.

"No." I began to walk away.

"Now wait a minute, what is the rush? You are not with

anyone, just give it a try." He urged on.

"No, I am just looking around." I said looking away.

"Well I guess you're too short to even get the ring into the first bottle anyway." I raised my eyebrow as he laughed at his own joke. Oh what the heck I thought. I walked up to him and reached my hand out for the rings. His smile widened in victory. I tossed the first ring and missed. The second and third rings missed too. He handed me three more. "Come on your not that short."

"I'm just distracted that's all." I said, then paused and looked at him. I didn't notice how incredibly gorgeous he was, with long light hair that fell in his face, he had big brown eyes. He was very fit too.

"Stop looking around and just concentrate. You're barely even looking at the bottles! "

Another round later I reached out with one word. "Again."

"Who you watching out for?" he asked. Staring me down now.

"No one give me more," I replied determined to get a ring over the bottle and not look at him again.

"Focus, you are all tense and flustered."

"Ok, ok." I closed my eyes and took a deep breath. "Focus Riley." I whispered to myself.

"You don't give up do you girl?"

"Never," I replied and tossed the ring. He screamed out loud in joy of my victory. "Wow see all you had to do was focus, you've earned this." He picked up a big stuffed animal and threw it at me. I looked down at the big brown bear and decided to name him Barry. I glanced up at him and we locked eyes, it scared me. I took my eyes off him, thanked him and started walking away. I knew making one ring in did not deserve this prize. I can feel his disappointed eyes on my back as I did. I was thirsty so I decided to go to a stand and buy a bottle of water. I noticed a middle aged couple was staring at me a few feet away. The moment my eyes laid on them I felt a strong but strange vibe. It was awkward and I didn't like it, the way they stared at me as if I had wronged them somehow. I returned the stares and looked around to see if there was anyone else they could be looking at. Then I started walking back to the place where I had left my friends.

The rest of the day I couldn't shake the couple out of my head, there eerie stares were so confusing, but I realized something else. I was different today, but just today. It was insane how just moments of looking at him and his smile made me smile too. It could really make my whole day. I was excited about everything. I wasn't bothered by the things that usually do. I thought that was all crazy talk and that someone couldn't make you happy and feel alive with a burst of energy. I believed it now. I was still hoping over time it would all go away and my stupid feelings would decrease and the effect he had on me would slowly disappear, but instead it got stronger and every day I realized more…

∞

15. A peace of mind

Things happened fast, at least in my life. It had only been two days since Paul had handed me his Bible. I was against it at first, I told him I couldn't take something he treasured so much with so many years of notes and highlights. He wouldn't let me leave the church unless it was with his Bible, so I took it. The same night I opened and started reading his highlights, that night by some miracle I slept peacefully. I felt a calmness when I opened this book, something none of the other books could ever do. I sat by the window every night and read verses and even prayed. I prayed for my friends and for Seth to be safe. I prayed for my peace... Even if it wasn't what I wanted; though I doubted I would ever get it. I prayed and felt a stronger force intervene, and I craved it every day. God helped me.

*

Seth seemed exasperated today.

"There claiming to be my parents and well I want you to meet them. I think you're the first person I wanted to know. Since we both did grow up together, wondering who they were." He focused his eyes at me waiting for an equally excited response from me.

"No actually I really haven't. I don't care." I replied wondering how his biological parents could have found him.

"Liar," he called me. He looked disappointed from my lack of enthusiasm.

"Seth I don't, I don't need anyone else in my life." We sat on my side walk in front of my apartment.

At first I couldn't read his expression, when he had bumped right into me on my way out for a jog. There was nothing, he seemed cautioned once he started telling me about them. But I didn't get it at first. It was just blank. I stared at him as he told me the little he knew about them. The whole time he spoke I had a strong urge to just gently caress his face. I was being hypnotized by his presence, just inches away, our knees almost touched but they didn't, I focused on his lips that spoke words.

"I don't know Seth, it seems a little weird. Didn't they tell us it was suspected they died in an accident?" I said before looking away to watch an airplane in the sky. I could tell he really wanted to know if this was all true, and he never really cared about anything. I took a deep breath and looked at him again, the cold magnetic bubble in my gut made it hard to breathe.

"What have they said? Like why did they have you there?" I hoped for some justifiable reason but it was that same story. They were young and had no money.

"For twenty years? They couldn't find you for that long? It must be kind of weird." And how were they presumed dead?

"Yeah it was awkward, but it's whatever I am used to disappointment in my life, I am ok with this falling apart."

"What do you mean?" There was a pause.

"We broke up." He peered down at the cement stairs.

"Aw no Seth, I am so sorry, why does that keep happening?"

He shrugged his shoulders.

"Why?" I asked.

"It just didn't work out."

"Are you sure you are ok?"

"I am fine," he replied. I got the strong urge once again. *Stop it*, the voice in me ordered. I just wanted to let my fingertips linger on his face, but I couldn't. Instead I moved an inch away on the cement. Glad that he didn't notice.

"You loved her though right?"

"Yeah." Suddenly both of us became silent and it felt very awkward so I decided to keep the conversation going.

"Back to this couple, do what you think is best but just be careful. Remember I am here always."

"I know thanks Rie." He smiled looking at me now.

"You hungry?" I asked.

His eyes all lit up, like a kid again.

"Come on, I got leftovers from last night."

"Yes! You know I love food Riley!"

You should be happy, he is single.

No I am not happy, I am upset, because he is upset. I just want him to be happy. She let him go, how could she, how could anyone? What made everything harder in my head was the hope I desperately tried to ignore or make disappear, had now just doubled and it hurt. I had enough illusions of him loving me by some miracle. I repeated over and over that this was not going to happen and I needed to crush every ounce of hope that popped into my brain. Every thought, image, scene or dream.

*

My life wasn't supposed to be exciting or dramatic. I never asked for that. All I ever dreamed was for a fair life full of trust, passion and honesty. I got the passion part a little too strong. Maybe my passion turned into obsession. I was never honest to anyone, I think it is best to just tell people what they want to hear, and it makes life a whole lot easier. There was barely any honesty in each face I crossed. My idea on life had turned around and laughed at me. Fair? Try the complete opposite. Every day I had to ask myself why some things couldn't just be fair and I couldn't believe how life threw trust at me, but there was things life could never stop me from having, and that was being strong. I believed I had faith that no matter the odds there would be an ending somewhere in this lifetime. Happily Ever After, I would get it, somehow, somewhere; I would never let my faith go. The key was just believing. I can't imagine a life where I didn't believe in anything.

I knew when my eyes laid onto the middle aged couple beside Seth. A bad feeling in my gut came over and I needed to find out why, they didn't look right, this wasn't what I imagined. And I had sketched them out even in my imagination more them my own parents. I could never stare in the mirror and try to make out what my family could have looked like, but I could look at Seth and imagine them so vividly. I really didn't want to know about myself, I was not interested in a disappointment like that. I had no need for it either. I never felt I was missing something; my family was the friends I grew up with.

We had talked about trying to find information on our birth parents. We had decided against it. We really never felt we needed anyone else. We did grow up in an orphanage, no one ever wanted to have us. Even if there was any family out there. The first time we weren't wanted was because the couple's that came in wanted little kids that resembled them and that was impossible for us by their red or blond hair and freckled skin. Then the rest just wanted babies. It was too late for us. Like if we were dogs in a kennel, everyone just came for the puppies, but we didn't pity ourselves for it. I didn't want to be separated from Seth ever; that hurt too much to think about.

Spence and Jane Throne? What kind of last name was that? Seth Throne, It sounded okay but I felt I had to keep repeating it to myself. Something wasn't right with it. "Riley my dear, what are your plans for the near future?" "Um, I-"

"I mean what do you want to do with your life, your career. You cannot work at the insurance office forever."

"I am still undecided that is all, I mean I have a lot of hobbies but I haven't had that big moment where I am so sure of what I am going to do."

"Oh that's no good at all, you should have known in high school." Jane said looking me up and down.

"Why?" I asked, trying to remember not to talk too much, even though I knew I could never make a good impression if my life depended on it.

"Well because in life you'll never know what opportunities will come to you."

"Yeah Riley," Seth said across the table sarcastically. We locked evil eyes for a second.

"You should be prepared for them." She continued, and then took a bite of her food acting very proper.

She had long blond hair that looked like it had been dyed repeatedly. Her nose appeared as if it had been poked several times too, I think everything else was real, she had light skin and her eyes were sort of blue. I couldn't tell with her big black glasses. "So where do you live Riley?"

"Oh just a small apartment by that big library, I live alone with my dog."

"Yes I know, - I mean, I heard." Spence added.
He shrugged his shoulders.

Weird, I thought to myself.

Spence had brown eyes and the black hair that Seth had, but it was long not short. It all still didn't look right though. I was really bothered that I didn't feel for them the way I always knew I would. Seth said something funny and made them laugh. It was hard to pay all my attention on them when so much was going through my mind. I couldn't shake the feeling off but I really had no idea what I could do about it. Why couldn't I figure out what was wrong with them, or if I should tell Seth what I thought. I wasn't sure what to do. The whole dinner was very odd and played out. For the first time I really did not want to be in the same room as Seth.

I sat down with my laptop and stared at the screen. I didn't expect to find anything, but I felt I had to at least try. I first closed all the annoying pop up ad's before typing in the search bar.
Spence and Jane Throne.
I waited for the page to load, no results. I tried the names differently a few times and then tried *Seth Throne,* still nothing. I stared at the screen for a countless minute and then decided to type in something more.
Car accidents in New York 1997.
There were three viewable results, one of an accident involving 6 teenagers, another a couple and two kids; and then one involved two teenagers that died from a car accident from being intoxicated while driving. I couldn't see any more information. I went back to the Google search engine and typed in *Ms. Woods's orphanage.* I got a picture of it with her standing on the steps of the building. I clicked on it and found a website where you could see what kids attended there or ever did. I searched for us; I clicked on Seth's name with his info. I thought how cruel, I didn't even want to click on mine. I exited the page with no answers and closed the computer.

∞

16. Never Ending Dreams

I already knew this was that same kind of dream. The one where I am at the breaching point of believing I am not in a dream… and then I wake up. That would happen maybe once a week or sometimes every two weeks. This was one of them, it would be different though, and they all were. I just knew the beginning, middle and end. The only thing I didn't know was how it would happen. What my illusion would become. How pathetic I would act or what the voices would say to me. What he would say to almost change my mind. My stronger side would yell at me to stay in reality. These would never end and the message in them was so clear to me. I knew there was only one way to stop them; by making the haunting nightmares actual reality, but that wasn't happening. She would never let it, so instead of letting the continuous dreams torment me I let them amuse me instead.

I found it pretty fascinating how my mind could work. I saw myself standing and pleading with someone, at first it was blurry but then everything came into focus. Seth was laying on a couch. This place did not seem like the orphanage, but where ever we were, we lived here. I stood beside the couch and I began to speak.

"Seth, umm you could at least talk to her once in a while. She did love you. Maybe still does. She misses you a lot."

I already knew I was referring to Ivy, but why? Why was I trying to help her? Why was I even talking about anyone else in my dream? I flashed my eyes at him, he laid there careless and was staring at his cell phone. I examined this room. I knew I shouldn't for even a second think I wasn't dreaming, because I had never seen this place. The whole room was blue; everything was blue; the doors, picture frames, and even the walls. I glanced down and saw that the carpet was royal blue and so was the T.V and book shelf. I looked over at Seth again and he turned his back to me on the couch. I got the hint. I stared at him for another moment and then said goodnight. I slowly walked away and into a gray hallway and then into another room, this one was red. I could tell by everything in it that this was my room. It was almost the same as his room; every part of the room was red. I laid down disappointed and slowly began to fall asleep. The room was freezing. I shivered repeatedly but liked the cold, when I felt I was about to fall into a deep sleep. I was startled and opened my eyes wide. Now alert to the sound of my name being called.

"Riley", it was Seth yelling my name in an upset tone.

"Come here now!" I jumped up and ran over to his room. He sat on the blue carpet now and was staring at the wall with his back to me.

"What's wrong, what is going on?"

He started to whisper in a disturbed tone now.

"I always wanted and thought that my happy endings... would be with..."

I stood confused when I shouldn't be; I examined the wall too.

Don't let it start. The voice warned.

The way he had spoken really made me think about what he said.

He is doing it on purpose.

"Me?" I asked staring at his back.

"For how long did you think this way, like for the past couple of years, how long Seth? What exactly do you mean?"

He wouldn't look at me.

"Seth I am confused!"

You are going frantic, SHUT UP! The voice in my head yelled.

"No, Seth how long, please talk to me!"

I had lost my grip on reality, just by the way he had spoken to me. This is a dream; I might as well do what I want.

"This is a dream, this is a dream!" I started to repeat my words in a cry.

Stop talking to him!

"I will wake up, this is a dream."

He turned around now with his soft confused expression. I felt a wave in my direction of its power. He stood up and walked to my side, I backed up into a blue wall but he still ended up by my side, holding his expression and my eyes.

"Answer me, because I need to tell you something!" I said grabbing him by the arm. I had lost myself; I don't even know who was telling him this, me or the voice.

"This is not real Seth."

"I know," he replied.

"There's something I am hiding from you!"

214

"I know," he said again.

"No you don't!"

Stop answering him.

"This is just a dream, something is going to wake me up."

"Will you stop saying that, you're freaking me out." He said coming closer.

This is weakening you.

"No, you know! Stop it Seth."

"I do."

"No, you don't, that I... "

"I do too Riley!"

He still looked confused and I was beginning to get frustrated.

"I'm going to wake up soon, I promise!" I said again, and again.

I got a warning in my gut, so I ran, I ran down the gray hall, and passed a brown room and then a green room. I opened the door to another room and slid in slamming the door behind me.

I shut my eyes hard, this room was white. Everything was a bright white just like the others. The florescent beams above me were strong. This was a bathroom. I sat on the cold white tile and hugged my knees.

Good girl, he cannot find you now. The voice in me said.

I started rocking back and forth still whispering to myself that this was all just a dream.

"Hey shut up, shut up Riley!" I whined at myself looking up.

He was there bent down to me on his knees. I wasn't sure how he got in here. The door was still locked.

"Calm down I'm serious." Came his sweet voice again. I could not fall for it.

"Liar go away, stop!" I yelled hiding myself again. I covered my ears but could still hear the voices.

215

"I am sorry. I know it is stupid and easy to do, but it is useless. It would just ruin the little thing I didn't even have with you, but it is ok. I'm going to wake up so it doesn't matter, that's how it works so don't even listen to me."

"I love you Riley, I love you!" He said shaking me.

Stop it you are nothing to him. The voice reminded me.

"Riley, I want to spend my life with you." He begged.

I hoped he wasn't aware of his power. My face was red and my eyes were puffy.

"I only love you Riley," he held my face with his hands. I calmed my voice and now spoke firmly and slowly.

"Seth you're going to leave me, you'll hate me and think I am stupid. You could never trust me now. I have lied to you too long." I closed my eyes and moved my head away from him. I began to hear loud music play. It was blaring through the bathroom, the loud music rumbled through my body.

"Ouch, stop it!" I clutched my stomach. "It hurts. Please, just go! I don't need you anymore."

I covered my ears but the music did not get any softer. I felt the rising pressure in my stomach.

"Get out! Don't come back!" I shouted again in the air to myself. He still begged me and touched me. I wanted to tell him to stop and that it hurt but I couldn't. I jumped up and leaped to the toilet and threw up what looked like bile. Then everything was gone and I was once again in a bubble waiting for the next dream to come. Bye.

I heard the voice whisper.

"Until next time."

∞

216

17. Hunch

I had left her in my dreams. At least I think I did. The last time I heard her was in that dream. For now I was strong. Hopefully she would only come to me when I was weak…then there was my faith, which had gotten surprisingly stronger and was letting me live better. I was strong, stronger then I have ever been. Though no matter what I would always feel alone in a way, I had peace. That was enough to make me feel I could go on the way I did.

*

A bake sale for the youth group sounded fun to me; I started at the table that was empty, not even a table cloth on it. The sale started in half an hour. There was a few adults setting up some tables and chairs outside, so I started on the main table. I first put a pink table cloth down. Which annoyed me for about six minutes, I was not a fan of that color. I laid it out on the table and began spreading it across it. Seconds later I saw that dark hair and soft olive kin of Seth approaching. I had my hopes high of him showing up today. When I saw him it released the wonder and started up my nerves. I smiled just knowing he was here, his eyes opened and smile widened when he saw me.

"Well, look who it is, just in time!" I said with my eyes locked on his.

"Me? I know," he said gloating.

"Hey help me?" I asked looking at how slow it was taking to spread the table cloth now that he was here.

"Of course, so what's up?" He asked me.

"Nothing, you?" I replied trying to take his focus off of me.

"Just busy with work, and studying too... and getting to know my parents."

"That is good." I said, now placing the trays and containers on the pink table cloth.

"Yea," he said stretching out his word. He stood over me, almost a foot taller, with a tray in his hand.

"Oh no Riley, think fast!" He said in a whisper exaggerating as he pretended to drop a tray on me. He stopped in midair and gave me a funny smile.

The one that made my mind blank and confused. I laughed out loud, feeling my heart get heavy. I felt like I needed to clutch it from falling out. I stared at him seriously with squinted eyes. I could barely be serious with that smile on.

"Give me!" I reached for the tray and he held it back. I

smiled with my hand out. I motioned to him to hand it over. He held it even higher.

"Seth!"

"What's wrong Riley? Too short to reach me?" He said laughing at me.

"Noooo!" I jumped up and grabbed it. He chuckled.

"Ok now we need plates, cups, and napkins." I counted my fingers naming them off.

"Ok let's go." He gazed at me with the smile where he perked his lips to the side. I breathed out counting them again. We set up everything and in just a little bit of time we were done.

"Oh one more thing, can you pick this up?" I pointed towards a box in the closet.

"Why?" He asked.

"Just get it, I am looking for these place card things."

"Ugh, always using me! You just want to see me bend over don't you Riley?" I coughed out a laugh.

"That's my plan Seth." He lifted the box setting it down on the floor outside the door. I found what I was looking for and stepped out of the closet.

"Damn, this is heavy." He said lifting it back up in the closet.

I put my hands on my hips and watched.

"Aww is it too heavy for little Seth?"

He fake frowned at me throwing the nearest thing he could find, and took a tissue from a tissue box. It fluttered to the floor.

"Oh great." He said staring at the tissue. We both laughed.

"Come on Seth we are done here." We both started walking side by side down the back of the church.

"I love how dangerous you could be sometimes, that tissue

could have killed me." He gave me a dis-configured face.

"Whatever Riley."

"Aw did I hurt your feelings?" I said sarcastically.

He pouted, "I thought you were my friend."

"I am!" I exploded.

"Out of all my friends, you cannot play that line, ever!"
I saw him smile under his breath before he turned away
from me and walked away. I played along chasing after him.

"Seth! Seth stop! That's not fair, I'm your best friend!"

"Wait you are? I didn't know I had a best friend?"

"Ok well you're my best friend."

"I am?" He asked shocked.

"Ugh you're one of my best friends." He laughed and then
quickly picked up a tree branch and swung it in my
direction. I laughed faking pain.

"Ha-ha!" He shouted making sounds as he swung it at me;
he always stopped before he touched me.

I tried to stay serious and act annoyed like I would if
it were anyone else, but instead I smiled so wide it hurt and
the laugh slowly came out.

"Come on," I said grabbing the branch from him.

"What! You cannot do that, touching it is forbidden."

"Ha I touch a lot of forbidden things." He opened his eyes
wide.

"Really," he said almost impressed.

"Like what?" He asked curiously.

"Name it." I whispered walking away with a smile.

He ran up to me, "No really what?" He continued. I
got serious.

"I tend to want forbidden things a lot in my life." I replied
staring at his eyes knowing that I would have to look away

before showing him too much. Though I knew he really wasn't really looking. I stepped on his shoe and backed up.

"What was that?" He asked.

"You're it!"

"At what?" he laughed.

"At shoe tag."

"Did you just make that up?"

"Yup," I ran.

He ran after me and I ran almost hitting a wall.

"Got you!" He said really close to me stepping on my shoes. I glanced up but my hair was in my face. I looked like a witch. I kept smiling. He stuck his finger in my hair.

"Hello? Where did you go Riley?" He asked moving my hair around.

"I don't know," I whispered. He pushed my hair away.

"I got it thanks." I said fixing my hair. We were such kids still after all these years. I saw people motioning for us to come inside and that we were starting the sale.

This time I didn't say come on; I didn't want to leave this spot. I mean ….who cared about a bunch of cookies. My question was answered right when Seth jumped up, "Oh I want cookies!"

*

A week later at school I sat reading a book in an empty Latin class room. I got tense and alert from the person who had just walked in.

"Hey," he said swinging open the door and spinning into

221

the room. He sat on the desk in front of me. I laughed feeling the pressure in my stomach and goose bumps on my skin.

"What are you reading?" He asked snatching it from my hands.

"Hey! It's not a big one, just another fiction story." He opened it up skimming through the pages.

"Oh good not another of those rants that go on for weeks; like that one with the lame vampires."

"Hey! Stop it! It's an amazing story! One of the best stories I have read too."

"Yeah sure." He smirked.

"And there's so much more to it!"

He smiled more.

"Yes I know."

"How would you know?"

"Because Riley you told me everything about it."

"Oh yeah ha-ha. Great book." I said again with a sigh. By now I had forgotten what the book was about and it was still in my hands.

"Where's your friends?"

"Oh they left, I'm just bored now, don't have anything to do."

"That's a miracle."

"Why?"

"Well because you're usually always busy Seth."

"Yea things change." He started humming and moving his hands like he was playing the drums. I put my book down and tapped my fingers on the table following his beat while playing a fake piano. He got more into it and started playing the guitar. I switched to a fast violin. I felt like such an idiot. I stopped and so did he. I giggled too much.

He got up and started dancing where he now stood in front of the class. He pretended to be the teacher. Mocking what she taught.

"I don't think that's even Spanish Seth!"

"Come dance with me Riley."

"Ha, oh no way!"

"Ok, at least finger dance."

"Finger dance?" I said in a questionable tone. He walked over pulling my two index fingers up making them sway back and forth.

"See your finger dancing!"

"Did you just make that up?" I asked.

"Yep," he replied.

Seth started singing to his movement and my stomach filled with butterflies. He just never stopped being so great. I couldn't help but to laugh.

"I know I'm totally ruining that song." He said.

"No you didn't."

"Riley, you will cringe whenever you hear it on the radio now."

"Nope I will smile, because you just made it better."

He rolled his eyes at me.

I inspected the room and decided I wanted to sit against the wall instead. This chair was hurting and it was normal for me to change positions and spots when I was reading, so I did, snatching my book from Seth again. I sat down with my book against the wall and knees folded in front of me. Seth froze with that funny expression again with a hint of confusion. He followed me slowly and sat down too. He sat too close, way too close. I didn't care if he noticed, but I moved a few inches and smiled, talking to make it unnoticeable.

 I looked up and he was just smiling. He moved again, our knees now touching; his body heat clinging to mine in seconds. I moved again and so did he, with a hard force this time almost knocking me over.

"Stop it!" I snapped knowing my face was flustered.

"Why?" He asked bringing his face inches away from mine. My heart started skipping beats and I held my breath having trouble finding an answer.

"Because I don't like people so close!" I breathed out.

"Not even me?" He asked still to close, bringing his shoulder close to me. He slowly got closer as if he were going to crawl on me. I put my hands up gasping and he laughed sitting back down.

"Especially you!" I said to loud.

 He showed me his fake offended expression. He frowned asking again why.

"You're over powering beauty is too much for my fragile self to handle." I laughed as I said it.

"That's the best excuse I have ever heard, because sometimes I cannot even handle myself. Do you have a mirror?"

"Why?" I asked.

"Just give me one."

"Ok." I said reaching into my bag.

"Here," I said. He opened it staring in with a smirk.

"Yes I see why you cannot sit too close." I laughed taking the mirror a way and I play punched him in his arm.

 He did too, but stopped before touching me. I kept smiling as we sat there in silence. I looked around the room and read a few lines to myself in Spanish. Next to the board was a dramatic picture of an old popular book.

I decided to start up an act to break the quiet room.
"Oh mi amor! Ven Salvame."
Seth got up laughing and prancing around the room.
"Oh my, I would help you, if I only could understand what you are saying."
"Porque no puedo, no está solo. Mi amor, por favor no vayas. Te quiero."
I whispered to him in Spanish, so grateful he did not understand, though it would not matter if he did. He laughed and ran back to me in slow motion on purpose. If anyone else did it I would think they were stupid but even his silliness was perfect.
"What did you just say? It was like hearing gibberish."
"Aw too bad you don't understand, oh well I'll just die."
"NO!!! Just tell me what you said."
"Never," I replied.

*

I noticed it right away. Seth was no longer with her. It did not give me hope he would now somehow want me. But because I think now maybe he would at least pay attention to me. It was easier to be myself when he wasn't with her. He would be with me and not want to be somewhere else. I should have known though, it would not last, because just a month later, he was with her again. I was happy, because he was, I could tell by the way he talked. Though I had no right to be unhappy for him. I also felt like something had been stolen from me as well. Three days went by and I was consumed with my disappointment. I wanted her back, the part of me full of strength, I needed it to keep me grounded. To keep me in reality, I fell into my fantasies to easily.

I asked her to come back, that I needed her and I knew I was crazy to argue with myself like this. It had to be unhealthy. I wasn't going to focus on that, if he was with someone or not, either way it wouldn't change my actions, I just had to deal with it. I could only be his friend. I couldn't disappoint him, I had promised him I wouldn't. I couldn't let him down by something as foolish as my overwhelming feelings for him. But I got to see him more, and he was happier when alone. I wished he would notice that.

I just needed to know she was there. I was afraid I would do something wrong or make a mistake, but how would I know she was here. I watched the page load. I knew exactly how I could know if she was here, I clicked to the page of pictures that I had seen a few times before. They say face your fears and seeing Seth in all these pictures, so happy, I knew that had to be facing them somehow.

I clicked the first album, and felt the pain, the heaviness and the feeling as if I was holding my breath, but I wasn't. I went picture after picture until I heard her voice.

WHAT ARE YOU DOING?

Turn that off and move away from the computer!
I clicked the box with the X, and stared at the screen.
I felt my eyes swell up and I cried. I cried because he was the only one that could get to me or break me.
After a while I opened up a new window and skimmed over the page of accidents in 1997 again.

I hoped it would distract me. I scrolled through and read the story of the two drunk teenagers, there was a picture and all the info on where they lived and the rest of

226

their family as well. I exited out of that page and skimmed through a bunch more until I came across the accident with six young adults. It seemed the most interesting out of them all. There was no alcohol and they didn't crash into another car.

It had just lost control; I clicked on the link that led me to some names. Three couples, the Jacobs couple, the Dawson's and the third couple was the Thorington's. My eyes blinked, rereading it again. Four people dead, but one couple survived, I clicked the images of the accident. Mostly just of cops and caution tape.

Then there was one of a car, so totaled you wouldn't think anyone could have ever survived. The next picture showed a few body bags. I counted four, but where were the two that were still alive? I skimmed through more until I found one of a woman looking pale as ever, hiding under a big jacket. She had a busted nose and lip. I scanned the image of the woman, her hair uncolored, light brown with young eyes.

There was no doubt that was her, just so much younger and innocent. The boy next to her with his back turned away from the camera. The girl staring into the picture was the same woman who stared at me when I bought my water at the fair. Why had they watched me? My eyes widened as I realized who this woman was. My heart started beating faster. Why had they changed their appearance and last name? I felt a wave of frustration and fear hit me; I had to find out why.

∞

18. Happily Ever After

"Seth, Seth! I need to talk to you!" I said too fast into the phone.

"What?"

"I need to tell you about this crazy hunch I have."

"Riley calm down."

"No, Seth listen."

"Aren't you going to say hi?"

"What? Listen you'll probably think I'm crazy but!-"

He cut me off again, "Riley I am busy, my parents- I mean Spence and Jane are coming over, they insisted on it and I have to have this place clean. They even mentioned my house should be clean last time."

"And you care?" I asked.

"I don't know I have to go, I'll call you later,"

"Wait Seth-." The line went dead. I had to get over there. I was freaking out already and I didn't know if anything I guessed was true, but what if they were and planned on hurting him or something.

Ok breathe, calm down! You don't even know anything! You're exaggerating!

I had to follow my instinct, I had to get to him. I couldn't even call for help, I had no evidence. I had such a horrible feeling something bad was going to happen. As I drove fast to Seth's apartment, using Kay's car that I had taken without asking. I kept calling him but no answer. I drove through the streets remembering a dream I had a few days ago, it had been flashes of images, and then that same backyard with the dog, cat and the play set. The big cherry tree and the smell of peanut butter and vinegar in the air.

There I was chasing a boy; a voice behind me yelled. "What are you doing?"

"It's him I know it is I have to find him." I said over my shoulder. Our voices echoed. I chased the boy, but for some reason it was all in slow motion. I reached for him but there was some kind of stronger force around him that would not let me reach him.

I kept running, but I didn't get any closer. Then he disappeared around a corner. I turned and he wasn't running anymore, but he just sat down with a disappointed expression. He was older now, he looked like he would if I saw him today. I called his name but he couldn't hear me. I started to run after him again, just to get a little closer, but then he was gone. I blinked swerving from hitting a car and pulled into his drive way. I jumped up but then realized I had not taken the seat belt off, I hit the seat growling. I unbuckled it and jumped out onto my feet and ran up the steps.

I banged on the door.

"Seth! I need you to open the door quick, let me in Seth!" I heard voices inside and I put my ear to the door.

"Oh that stupid girl is here, could never get rid of her, huh?" I heard Spence say loudly.

"What? Riley's not stupid, you don't even know her."

"I'm sick of this, let's just tell him." Jane said farther away.

"Tell me what? What's going on?"

"Seth!" I yelled into the door again banging on it.

"Where are you going, son sit back down?"

"But Riley—"

"No. Sit."

"What the hell!" I heard Seth's muffled voice yell. There was a big crash. A lamp I think.

"What are you doing? Are you crazy?"

I had to get in there! His spare key!

He was always losing his keys so he had spares. I looked around and between things. My heart was racing and adrenaline going wild. I could barely reach above the door. My dumb shortness was no good right now.

Under the mat? Ha of course Seth, the most obvious place. I opened the door and ran in. Seth sat on his couch, with his confused expression, though this one wasn't so hot. He couldn't see what I did, Spence held a long sharp kitchen knife behind his back. Jane was not there but I could hear things being thrown everywhere in the next room. None of them noticed me.

They both just argued.

"Where is it?" He yelled at Seth.

"Where's what?"

"The money boy!"

"What money?"

"Your father hid it from us and put it under your name. It's mine; I did most of the stealing anyway that son of a bitch had no right. So I got rid of them, all of them. I know you must have been told about the security box." Seth still sat there confused but I could tell he was angry.

"You're not my parents? I don't understand," Seth replied looking up at Spence bewildered.

I made my move, jumping on his back loosening his grip on the knife. Seth was now fully aware of the danger that came from my horrible effort to keep him down.

"Get off me!" He roared.

I was thrown across the room and hit a table. My head felt suddenly heavy and a sharp pain struck through my brain. I touched my head trying to steady myself. Boney hands began to pull on my hair and throat to hold me down. Spence shouted in anger and wrestled with Seth.

The knife was no longer on the floor. I tried to get away but I felt the sharp pain of a screw driver digging into my neck. Spence banged Seth's head into the table and I screamed out.

Seth swung a crystal vase at his hand and he fell back onto the floor, but he got right back up with the knife in his hand. I didn't care about the pain in my neck or head.

I fought to get away. "Seth!" I pointed and bit down on Jane's arm. She cussed and let go. Seth turned and kicked Spence in the leg twisting the weapon out of his hand and jamming it into Spence's body. He fell to the floor with the knife in his side. I froze and breathed out in relief. Jane gasped and made a run for it. She started for the door but I grabbed her and punched her right in the nose.

My hand felt like a bowling ball had fallen on it. I guess it worked, she collapsed to the floor banging her head against the tile floor and passing out.

"Oh fuck, Seth, are you ok?" I ran over to him, pausing a little by the dizziness and pain in my head. I got to him still convinced he was intact. Both of us breathing heavily and not sure what to do.

"I'm fine, thanks to you, you saved my life Riley."

"Well of course, I love you." I froze on the last word. What did I just say? I said that aloud.

"I love you Seth." I said it again, what was wrong with me? I eye balled him, he was frozen too, speechless. I had told him I loved him before. What was giving it away? Was he just in shock after stabbing someone?

Say something that's the problem right now. You're telling him by not saying anything!

I turned away, the expression on his face made me regret blurting that out. Were we both in shock at what had just happened. It was the adrenaline, I didn't even know what I was saying. I gazed up at him and his expression was changing.

"Oh shit," was all I got out before I screamed again.

I saw an object coming down and slamming into Seth's head.

He fell to the floor limp and unconscious.

Spence with the knife still in his side slid to the floor again.

I could hear sirens and yelling around me. Everything went blurry. I shrieked and bent down to him. There was blood coming from his head. I looked at it in my hands. I started to tremble. A few long minutes went by, I heard the paramedics trying to talk to me as they put him on a stretcher. I saw police officers checking for pulses and cuffing Spence and Jane.

Was I losing my best friend? He was so still in my arms. I tried to get up and follow them but felt a wave of nausea come over me and I felt myself slowly falling down to the floor, and then everything went dark.

*

It had been three days since the incident, two of those days Seth laid unconscious. I had been there those two days praying he would wake. They were the worst days of my entire life. I was positive. I couldn't lose him, not this way. He laid in the hospital bed with his eyes closed and so still. It scared me when he napped now, I was afraid he would go into a coma again. I sat beside him as his eyes fluttered open. I breathed out in relief to see him look at me.

"Hey," I said touching his shoulder lightly. He had suffered from a concussion as well. I had been too worked up to notice the wound on my neck from the screw driver Jane had stabbed me with. Which is why I had passed out at the scene. I stared at him wondering how much he remembered. He told the officers he did not remember much after Spence banged his head into the table. At least that's what he says. He did not seem to recall what happened after. Including what I had blurted out by mistake when I had went into shock from the attack. It turns out I had hit Jane so hard I had almost broken a knuckle. My hand was bandaged up to help the pain. He looked at me like he always did. Nothing hinted that he remembered what I said. I mean I almost didn't believe it. It was a mistake and I was caught up in the moment. I remembered the conversation I had with the officer when I made my statement that night in the hospital.

"You don't have to keep visiting me you know, I'm ok." He said clearing his throat and looking around the room. His head was wrapped with a bandage.

"I know I have just been waiting for a good time to tell you something." I replied noticing his eyes widen.

"I found out some information about them, it turns out there last name is really Thorington. Not Throne. They were involved in a car accident with two other couples. It looks like our parents were the ones that died in that crash. They knew each other Seth, our parents were thieves. I said it as if I was still trying to believe it myself. We could have known, all the information was there. I'm starting to believe that fire at the orphanage wasn't a mistake either. For some crazy reason Spence thought there was money your father kept from him."

I could tell he was upset to hear he had been duped. He had really believed they were his parents.

The door to the room opened and a man walked in. He seemed as if he was in his late fifties. He wore a suit and walked slowly.

"Can I help you?" I asked looking cautioned.

"Actually you can, I am here to see you two."

"Us?" I asked looking at Seth.

He shrugged.

"My apologies, I'm detective Rodriguez, well retired actually. I just push papers around sometimes. But I saw your case come in and I recognized some names involved and could not believe the coincidence. I had to come see for myself."

"I don't understand." I peered at him curious now.

"I worked on that case, almost 20 years ago. It was during my first year as a detective." He replied taking a seat in one of the chairs across from us.

I sat down too.

"You kids sure grew up fast. You're lucky, that man would have killed you both. He's insane. Mr. Jacobs and you to Ms. Dawson."

I flashed my eyes at him choking on my words.

"Riley" —I cut him off. "I am Riley, that's Seth."

He continued, "Wow I can't believe you two are still together. Sorry, it's just most kids never know anyone after they leave the orphanage."

He paused for a moment.

"Well to answer some of the questions you probably have, yes it does appear both of your parents were together with the Thorington's. They conned people of their money, but we didn't find any money or evidence to prove Spence Thorington crashed that car on purpose that night. But that whole accident seemed so suspicious to me, I couldn't shake it for weeks. Something was off about them and how they barely had a scratch."

"Where were we when it happened then?" Seth asked him. He looked a lot more perked up now. I was going into shock again. I blinked several times to snap out of it.

"Together actually, you probably wouldn't remember but you were being watched by your grandmother Riley. She had wanted to take care and raise you both; but she was too ill. The state could not allow it with her condition, she died not too long afterwards. I'm sorry." He added

"Wait me? I had a Grandmother?" I asked surprised.

"We have an address to a little house where she lived her whole life. It is abandoned now, no one wanted to live in that old place. Here," he said passing me a piece of paper with an address on it.

"You both might want to just stop by, the house was a cute little thing. Mrs. Mar Dawson; I am told she was a great old thing. I remember she had a lot of visitors before she passed away too." He got up from his seat as he spoke.

"Ha. Well look at that, we knew each other, want to go?" I asked looking at Seth.

"Of course Rie," He replied. Seth seemed in a better mood now that we had some answers.

*

The house was small and definitely abandoned, but it had this angelic look to it too. I felt a radiating warmth around it just by being there. I took note of a path of brown stones that led to the door. The path was so old there were patches of missing stones. There was a small fountain rusted and drained of water. I knew birds had once drank and bathed in it though. Cobwebs and dust covered the steps and door. By the door was a window and a small metal bench in front. People once sat there and watched the neighborhood over the long bushes along the steps.

"Seth, doesn't this place look so familiar?"

"But we have not been here since we were babies and I am older then you. I would remember this place more not you." He looked around trying to grasp a memory. He now had a small bandage on his head. He wore a long sleeve green sweatshirt and jeans.

I stared him down for a long minute.
"I know but it seems so familiar." I replied snapping out of it and looking away. I touched the walls, feeling the peeled beige paint on my fingertips.
"It's locked." He said trying to turn the knob a few times. I frowned disappointed.
"There is a fence I think, let's try the fence." We both walked around the front of the house and over to the metal wired fence. He pulled the latch up and pulled the squeaky gate open.
There was the first thing I saw that made me gasp and jump up.
"What? What is it? Riley the doctor said to stay calm and walk slow."
"That tree!" I gasped again.

I ran forward and saw a huge old tree, a swing set, a seesaw and an orange slide. The shed that once had a dog chained to it. The empty table that the cat had laid sleeping on. The tree had no cherries, which was sad. I would have liked to try one. The grass was a little yellow and empty dog bowls lay on the grass, one turned over.
"Wow," I breathed out.
"That's amazing." I listened to the wind chimes that still hung around the yard.

"I can't believe it, how you remember?" He gazed at me in awe.
"I don't. I swear I dreamt this place Seth, I don't remember being here, but I remember this dream very clearly." We stood there for a while and explored the place the best we

could. My only other discoveries was a bucket by the patio and an old map beside it. A few dead herb plants and a bird house hanging from another tree.

"Come on. We can go now Seth."

He nodded in agreement and we made our way back to the front of the house.

"You sure you're ok?"

"Yesss! Just like I have been ok the seven times you asked already."

I turned away blushing. Hoping no memory had come to him over the past few days.

We walked around and he got in the driver seat of his car. I spotted an older women across the street. "I'll be right back ok," I said already skipping off.

"Ok," he replied from behind me. I could tell he was playing with his phone.

I walked over to the short woman with gray hair; she appeared to be in her late eighties.

"Excuse me, hi." I said the way I did when I was talking to strangers.

"Can I ask, how long have you lived here?" She looked up at me, suddenly startled and stared at me for a long time. I waved my hand in the air.

"Hello?"

"I, I know you!"

"You do?" I got excited.

"Those bright blue eyes, so light they are almost silver."

"You knew my Grandmother?"

"Yes! She was my dear friend, she was such a lovely woman, and everyone loved her. I never thought I would see you again. Not after they took you from her. The woman stood

238

looking me down. Her eyes were glowing now. Come, come I think I have something that belongs to you." She said giving me a big hug and showing me into her house. She smelled like cigarettes, sweat and a food spice I couldn't seem to figure out. I followed her in, this house was also small, and it had old dusty furniture and the smell of Latin food being cooked. She disappeared into another room and appeared with a small burgundy velvet music box in her hands. She handed it to me. I opened the box and a soft melody filled the room, it sounded like a very old children's song. Inside was a small necklace covered in dust. I picked it up and blew off the dust. From the dust came a sterling silver ancient chain with a pendent heart.

I smiled, "This was hers?"

"Yes," she replied nodding. "And I know Mar would want you to have this."

I wiped my finger over the heart to notice small letters engraved in the silver.

True Love Waits. I rolled my eyes at the coincidence.

"She loved you so much; her only grandchild. There was also a boy I remember, cute little thing; ran around you in circles when you could barely stand up yet. She loved him as if he was her own blood too." She reached into the box; at the bottom laid a small picture of who I knew right away was Mar Dawson. My Grandmother, I was maybe two and she held me in her arms and beside her was the little boy I still knew, with his blue, blue eyes staring into the camera. "She used to joke about how one day you two would end up together."

I smiled, of course. She would know.

"She had so much wisdom and love in her, everyone was

drawn to her."

"Thank you." I hugged her again.

"Oh I am sorry, I am Sindy by the way."

"Well it was nice to meet you."

"Likewise, young one, come visit anytime." I walked out of the house holding the picture, necklace and the music box. Seth was dancing in his seat and singing real loud to the radio. I felt a connection with my grandmother and was happy to know all this about her. I actually had someone else besides Seth. I put the picture and necklace away when I noticed a hidden flap at the bottom of the box. I pulled it up and below was a small key. Like the ones banks used. My eyes widened. I walked to the car slowly trying to take everything in.

I knew when I held Seth in my arms and felt his blood on my hands. When I thought I was going to lose him I realized something. Unrequited love wasn't so bad. Because all that really mattered to me was that he was happy. That he was alive. As long as that was true I would be just fine. I could deal with it.

Some people say you never know what you got till it is gone, but I did know and that's why I wasn't letting it go. I would not ruin what we had over feelings. Even my Grandmother thought we belonged together and I knew if what I believed about true love was real, and that it did last forever and if it was meant to be all the pieces would fall into place. Love should require patience anyway. Maybe someday, when he reads this tale of a girl that dreamt of him. When he reaches this last page, maybe; just maybe he will understand a fraction of how much I cared for him. That's all I wanted.

So as I get into this car I am getting in knowing I am a friend. A friend that had a purpose in his life. The way it is supposed to be, at least in this life anyway. But there was one thing I was sure of. And I can admit it now. I am a dreamer and this is my secret.

∞ I Love Seth. ∞

www.ingramcontent.com/pod-product-compliance
Lightning Source LLC
Chambersburg PA
CBHW050513260626
47157CB00004B/1302